STARS FOR THE TOFF

Stars For The Toff

JOHN CREASEY

Walker and Company

New York

CONTENTS

This book is for Olga Stringfellow,
who introduced me – and so the Toff –
to the stars.

A MAN AND HIS MAN

"Jolly," said the Honourable Richard Rollison.

"Yes, sir?" responded his manservant.

"Do you know a word which perfectly describes both you and me?"

Jolly, a man of many pauses and great deliberation, studied Rollison's face earnestly. In that sub-conscious way which old friends acquire, he saw the other as a kind of reflection of himself. There were, of course, marked differences. Rollison's eyes were clear and grey and fringed with upward sweeping lashes; Jolly's were brown and sad, their brightness only lurking, their lashes sparse. Rollison's face was that of a man younger by ten than his forty-odd years; a handsome one too; Jolly, who was sixty, could pass anywhere for seventy. Rollison's face was hardly lined and his handsomeness was heightened by the bronze of Alpine winter sunshine; Jolly's face was pale and wizened.

"You're taking your time," remarked Rollison.

"You are a difficult person to describe, sir. May I ask whether you mean a physical description?"

"No. A description—" Rollison hesitated, then

beamed as if a *bon mot* had sprung to his mind —"a description which sets our age and our place in this unhappy world."

After another pause, Jolly asked: "How many letters, sir?"

Rollison's face dropped.

"You know very well that I can't spell."

"I know you enjoy pretending that you can't, sir. A description which sets our age and our place in this world. Ah. Let me see." Jolly screwed up his eyes as if praying to an oracle, while Rollison watched him affectionately; there had never been a time when he had not known Jolly.

Jolly opened his eyes very wide.

"Anachronistic, sir?" he hazarded.

Rollison laughed.

"I should have expected it! You're as ready to face the facts of life as I am. Anachronistic it is indeed. We belong to yesterday. Perhaps even the day before yesterday. No man has a man today."

"Most unfortunate when true, sir," remarked Jolly.

"And no man serves another with the same unfailing loyalty as you do," observed Rollison. "Do you think there will ever be another like you?"

"There will certainly *never* be another gentleman like *you*, sir."

"Hm," said Rollison pensively. "We may both be right. The day of dudes and dukes and private eyes is past, this is an age of bugs and computers and brainwashing. Do you know what has prompted my near-nostalgic mood?"

"I think so, sir," said Jolly.

They both smiled as they turned their gaze upon the wall behind the large pedestal desk where Rollison sat much of most days. On this wall were the trophies, as Jolly had come to call them, of the hunt; so it was known as the Trophy Wall. On it hung a strange assortment of objects, from a poison phial to a pencil-pistol, from a bloodstained dagger once used to stab to a lip-sticked silk stocking once used to strangle. There was a preserved scorpion and a feather from the neck of a dead chicken; a torn glove; and the faded score of an old song sheet. Each was the trophy of a hunt, by Rollison, of a criminal—of a man who had killed. Each hunt had been successful and each exhibit told the story — why. Even the top hat, closest to the ceiling, two bullet holes drilled through the shiny nap of the crown, told a story: that hat, worn during an escapade nearly twenty-five years ago, had first earned Richard Rollison his soubriquet — the Toff.

It had since become famous in many parts of the world.

On the Trophy Wall were forty-nine exhibits — representative of the forty-nine men and women who had been brought to justice by the Toff. Some had been hanged; some (the later ones) were serving their so-called life sentences. Several, reprieved during the dole-ful days of hanging, were now leading outwardly happy and respectable lives.

"The next," said Rollison, "will be the fiftieth trophy."

"I was wondering, sir," said Jolly.

"Wonder on."

"*Need* there be?"

"A number fifty?"

"That is what I ask myself from time to time, sir."

"Jolly," said Rollison, "don't you believe in fate?"

"Not altogether, sir."

"Elucidate."

"Not if you mean you are *fated* to make yet another investigation, sir. I think it is within your power to stop it."

"I don't, Jolly."

"I cannot believe that all our actions are predestined," Jolly protested, with notable dignity. "We are surely masters of our own fate to some degree."

"You were born into service," Rollison reminded him.

"And stayed because I liked it, sir."

"Had you been born a bookmaker or a candlestick-maker, would you have spent your life with me?"

Jolly raised his hands a resigned inch or so.

"That is one of the imponderables."

"Yes, I know. So is fate. Jolly," went on Rollison, "do you believe in seers?"

"*Seers*, sir?"

"Those rare creatures supposedly gifted with second sight?"

"I don't think so, sir. Intuition, perhaps."

"No. Second sight."

"If I *have* to give an opinion – no, sir, I don't believe in them." Jolly looked a little uneasy as he answered, frowning. "Is there some particular reason for these questions?"

"Yes." Rollison moved across the large room, a combination of study and living-room, essentially a man's with its massive leather chairs and its sporting prints, its lack of any sign of femininity. He picked up a newspaper, the *Daily Globe*, flipping over the pages until he came to a photograph of a dark, gipsy-like woman with a shawl over her head and long, voluminous skirts. Her strange, almost hypnotic gaze stared up at him, absorbing all his attention, so that he scarcely noticed the young girl photographed beside her.

It was with a conscious effort that he at last wrenched his eyes from hers, and handed the newspaper to Jolly, who looked down at the photograph.

"And this is the reason, sir?"

Rollison nodded. "If you read the list of people this Madam Melinska is said to have swindled, you will see the august name of Lady Hurst. She —"

Jolly, appalled, cried out:

"Not Lady *Hurst*, sir?"

"No less."

"But *she* can't have been taken in by a charlatan!"

Rollison made no reply, and Jolly, after his first incredulous exclamation, studied the charges brought against the self-styled seer who called herself Madam Melinska. Convincing her clients of her ability to see into the future, she had, so the newspaper report read, persuaded them to give her certain sums of money for investment in a company known as Space Age Publishing, Limited. Of this money there was now no trace.

The police had made the arrest; and Madam Melinska, it was said, would be in the West London Magistrates Court to face the charge this morning.

It was now ten minutes past nine.

"Are you going to the Court, sir?" inquired Jolly.

"Not unless I'm invited or instructed to," said Rollison. "Have you read the small print?"

"Yes. That among the – ah – Melinska woman's clients who have invested money has been Lady Hurst. Do you expect her to ask you to take an interest in the case?"

"Yes," said Rollison. "I certainly —"

The telephone bell cut across his words. Rollison lifted his hand palm-outwards – an "after you" sign to Jolly, who took the receiver and answered in his quiet, modulated voice:

"This is Mr. Rollison's residence." There was a momentary pause, then a look first of alarm, then of resignation, flitted across Jolly's face. "Yes, my lady," he said. "Mr. Rollison is in."

Rollison, surprised at the extent of his own satisfaction, took the telephone with one hand and with the other signalled to Jolly to stay where he was. Before speaking, he sat on the arm of a brown leather chair and stretched out his long legs.

"Good morning, Aunt," he said, with mock deference.

"Richard." This was Lady Hurst at her most autocratic. "I wish to see you."

"Very well, Aunt," said Rollison. "When?"

"In half an hour's time."

"I'm sorry —" began Rollison, but before he could go on, his protest was brushed aside in a torrent of command from his oldest surviving relative and the one member of his family for whom he had regard, affection and respect. This was a matter of great importance; he must drop everything else and give it priority. It was not often that his aunt requested a favour and on this occasion he *must* grant it.

" . . . so be here in half an hour's time, Richard," she ended, as if it would never occur to Rollison to insist on "no".

"But Aunt Gloria —"

"*Be* here, Richard."

"But Aunt Gloria!" cried Rollison, in convincing mock distress, "I can't be both with you *and* at the West London Magistrates Court, can I?"

There was a curious sound at the other end of the telephone as if Lady Hurst had suddenly caught her breath. Jolly gave a wan smile and moved towards the domestic quarters, while Rollison winked at the Trophy Wall and pictured his aunt's stern, deeply-lined face in his mind's eye. He waited in the long silence, until Lady Hurst said in a very positive tone:

"So she *was* right."

"Who was right and what was she right about?" demanded Rollison.

"Madam Melinska was right," stated Lady Hurst flatly.

"Glory," said Rollison in his most winsome voice, "you're a darling, and the most generous and kind-hearted darlings sometimes get taken for a ride. How much have you lost?"

"One thousand pounds," answered Lady Hurst.

"You'll survive," Rollison said drily, "and why —"

"Be *quiet*, Richard!"

"Yes, Aunt."

"And listen to me. I was *not* swindled. I am not a senile old woman who throws her money away on confidence tricksters. I have managed my financial affairs in my own way all my life and I have made a better job of it than you."

"Yes, Aunt," said Rollison again, now genuinely meek; certainly his speculations on the Stock Exchange, some years ago, had cost him dear.

"Madam Melinska," began Lady Hurst, "is —" She paused, then went on with great vehemence —"is absolutely honest and trustworthy. She warned me that if I invested this thousand pounds I would probably be accused of criminal folly. I have been. She also told me that *she* would be accused of fraud. She has been. She told me that a tall, dark, handsome stranger —"

Rollison made a choking sound.

"— stranger, that is, to *her*," his aunt careered on, "would become interested in the charges *before* I made any attempt to enlist his help. She said that he would be a relation of mine —"

"But Aunt —"

"— and my only quarrel is with her use of the word 'handsome'," continued Lady Hurst. "She meant, clearly, that you would take notice of these absurd charges very quickly. You have. She also said that, with your help, the money I had lost would be repaid to me, not once but three times over, but that this would not happen straight away and I must be prepared to wait."

"Wait!" echoed Rollison hollowly, "My dear Aunt, you certainly *must* be prepared to wait. And wait a very long time. *Surely* you don't believe you'll ever see a penny of that money again?"

"I certainly do believe it," said Lady Hurst sharply. "Everything else Madam Melinska said has come true. She told me you'd take an unsolicited interest in the case, and you have."

Rollison sighed.

"But, Aunt, she could easily have known I've a reputation for poking my nose into other people's business. And once she knew you had a nephew *with* my kind of reputation —"

He paused, hearing his aunt breathe heavily into the receiver, and steeled himself against whatever blast she was preparing. With great deliberation and in her deepest voice, she responded:

"Richard, you are both a cynic and a sceptic. I shall now prove that you are *quite* wrong about her, and that she *does* have some strange gift of *seeing* facts of which she can have no personal knowledge. Go to your Trophy Wall, and count the number of trophies on it."

Rollison said faintly: "Yes, but—but why?"

"Go and count them!" his aunt thundered.

"I counted the trophies last night," Rollison told her defensively. "Jolly and I were in a nostalgic mood."

"Then you found, according to Madam Melinska,

that there were forty-nine, and that today you are to begin your fiftieth investigation." After a pause the old woman went on with a touch of anxiety in her voice: "Isn't that true, Richard? This *will* be your fiftieth case?"

"Glory be," said Richard Rollison sonorously, "that is exactly right. Fifty it is."

"But how could she know?" whispered Jolly, from the door.

2

MADAM MELINSKA

"Jolly," said Rollison.

"Sir?" said Jolly.

"When did this woman come here and count the trophies?"

"Never, sir, to my knowledge."

"Whom have you told?"

"No one, sir."

"Are you quite certain?" asked Rollison. "You might have just mentioned it to someone in passing —"

"Impossible, sir," said Jolly.

"How can it be impossible?"

"Until last night I thought there were forty-six trophies. I had made an error in my card index record several years ago."

Rollison caught his breath before saying, almost unbelievingly:

"So nobody *could* have known that the score was forty-nine."

"No, sir," Jolly concurred with simple positiveness.

The two men stared at each other without moving, Jolly looking like one who, having roundly declared that he did not believe in ghosts, now found himself face to face with one. They were so still, so silent, that the ticking of the French ormolu clock on the mantelpiece began to sound in Rollison's ears.

He moved at last, lifting the telephone again very slowly.

"Go and do whatever you have to do in the kitchen, and put your thinking cap on," he ordered. He dialled 230 1212 as Jolly disappeared; a slow-moving, puzzled Jolly. Almost as soon as he had stopped dialling, a girl said quite crossly:

"Scotland Yard."

"Superintendent Grice, please."

"*Who?*"

"Mr. Grice. Tell me," said Rollison, "is everything all right at the Yard this morning?"

"All *right!*" the girl exclaimed. "It's been bedlam. It's been — you're through."

A man with a reassuringly crisp voice said: "Grice."

"Good morning, Superintendent," said Rollison, brightly. "This is —"

"Good morning, Rolly," said Superintendent William Grice. "I hope *you* haven't called about Madam Melinska, too."

Rollison was momentarily stumped for words. During the pause which followed he heard Grice giving instructions; then, suddenly, Grice was back, still brisk, still clear.

"Sorry," he said. "I was on the other line when you rang."

"Bill," said Rollison, "what's this I hear about bed-lam at the Yard this morning?"

"Whoever told you that was right," said Grice. "We've been flooded out with calls from zanies and half-wits – half a minute." His voice faded, and Rollison pulled the newspaper towards him and once again studied the photograph of Madam Melinska. She must have been a beautiful woman in her youth, he decided, noting the high cheek-bones, the long, lean jaw, the proud tilt of the head. Now she was probably in her early sixties – but she was still beautiful for those who had eyes to see it.

After a moment it dawned on him that he had paid little attention to her companion. Her name, he read, was Mona Lister, and she was Madam Melinska's assistant. She had a pretty face, and fair, wispy hair hanging to her shoulders – but as he leaned forward to examine the photograph more closely, Grice came back on to the line.

"Sorry, Rolly – what is it you *do* want, anyhow?"

"I hardly dare tell you," Rollison said. "What time is Madam Melinska due in Court today?"

"So you *are* interested in the woman," said Grice, almost testily. "Around ten o'clock, I should say. But you haven't a chance."

"A chance of what?"

"Getting in. There's a half-mile queue outside the Court already, stretching from both ends of Southcombe Street. Uniform's had to detail thirty extra men to keep order. We've had twenty times the usual number of calls this morning, from threats of murder to threats of eternal damnation, as well as pitying souls who say we should know better than to try to stop the stars in their courses. *You* didn't lose any money over Melinska, did you?"

"My sainted Aunt Gloria did."

"*What?*" There was a moment of silence, then Grice gave a throaty chuckle and laughter quivered in his voice as he went on: "That's my best moment of the morning; I didn't think I'd laugh at anything today. But seriously — you won't get in."

"Not even disguised as a policeman?"

"No," said Grice firmly. "I shall *not* spirit you in. There simply won't be room." He paused for a moment, before asking in a puzzled way: "Did *you* realise what a fantastic public interest there was in astrologers and fortune-tellers?"

"I'm learning," said Rollison. "Thanks, Bill. See you in Court."

He rang off, and after a long spell of cogitation, went through a narrow passage and into the kitchen, where Jolly, resplendent in green baize apron, was neatly dropping crisp rings of onion into a flour-dusted dish.

"Ha, hot-pot," said Rollison.

"As I am not sure what time you will be back, sir."

"No. Grice says that Madam Melinska is attracting film-star crowds."

"So I would expect, sir. Have you any special instructions?"

"Yes. Find out if anyone has been here in the past few weeks who knows Madam Melinska or Mona whatever-her-name-is, and who can count up to forty-nine. Some people are natural counters of heads and trophies. I knew a man who never addressed a public meeting without estimating the number of victims in front of him, and —"

"Quite so, sir."

"It's time I went, is it?" said Rollison. "Very well. Expect me when you see me."

It was a rare, golden morning in May. The sun, bright and venturesome, found improbable gaps and cracks through which to penetrate. The milkman, the postman and somebody's daily help wished Rollison the best of good mornings. A day, he reflected, when it was good to be alive. The West London Magistrates Court in West Kensington was too far away to walk to, but parking would be impossible, and he turned out of Gresham Terrace towards Piccadilly and hailed a taxi; it stopped.

"Nice morning, Guv'nor!"

"What a happy place the world is this morning," remarked Rollison.

"For *some* folk," observed the taxi-driver, sagely. "Where to, sir?"

"As near West London Magistrates Court as you can get."

"I'll do my best, sir," said the taxi-driver. "But it may take some time. Just come from that direction, I have — never seen crowds like it, the streets are packed solid."

The taxi-driver was right.

The crowds stretched all along Southcombe Street, people standing five and six abreast, filling every corner and doorway, blocking the pavements and overflowing into the road. Most were women, but here and there a long-haired, Edwardian-trousered youth waited with the soul-starved patience of the empty-headed. There was no forward movement in the queue, and there was likely to be none, for the West London Magistrates Court was no different from other London police courts; the public gallery was large enough to take only a handful.

Rollison saw the extra police – six were standing close to the entrance. As he made his way towards it, a plainclothes detective from the Division approached him.

"You here on business?"

"Serious business," Rollison answered.

"*What* business?" The detective, big and burly, drew closer, and said *sotto voce*, "Nip in quick, Mr. Rollison." Aloud, he complained: "Why don't they tell me?"

Rollison went inside gratefully.

He knew the sedate manner of warders and policemen and court officials. It was traditional that there should be quietness if not complete silence. So it was now – except that by the door leading towards the public benches and the Press box an unusual crowd of eager-faced men and women muttered among themselves under the condemnatory gaze of two policemen and a magistrate's clerk. Over their heads Rollison saw a solid mass of people inside the panelled room, and constant movement where usually there was dull sedateness. A red-faced court policeman was struggling to keep some kind of order. Catching sight of Rollison, he drew a hand across his sweaty brow.

"Ever see the like, sir?"

"No, Sergeant, never. No room at the Court, eh?"

"Take my tip, sir, you go down into the cells and on up that way. When his nibs comes in he'll clear *this* mob away. Follow his nibs, sir, that's the safest thing."

"What it is to have friends," murmured Rollison appreciatively.

"We owe you a turn or two when we think of the number of prisoners you've put in the dock for us, sir."

Rollison thought: "It's a rewarding world, after all."

He went down the flight of steps the sergeant had indicated, and into the quietness of the room below. Here, a few prisoners and a few policemen sat or stood about, amongst them three solicitors of his acquaintance. One nodded. The third came up, a man whose name Rollison could not recall.

"Who's *your* client, Rollison?"

"Just a watching brief."

"Don't say Madam Melinska fleeced you, too, she's only *been* in this country a few months. Must be a quick worker, what?" The man laughed coarsely.

"Prejudgment?" murmured Rollison.

"Personal opinion. She's a smooth-tongued bitch."

"You're not appearing for her, I trust? Nor against her?" Rollison added hastily.

"No," the other answered.

"What do you know about the girl?"

"A chip off the old bitch."

Rollison winced.

"Mr. Godley!" a younger man called, and the man

with Rollison turned away, with a grunt which may have been "excuse me". Rollison watched him striding on stumpy legs towards the cells, and echoed in disgust:

"Godley, good God!"

Then an odd realisation came to him. He was angry with Godley for his condemnation of the two women.

As he assimilated this fact, a tall, grey-haired, austere-looking man came in at a side door: Nimmo, the stipendiary magistrate in charge. Ignoring everyone, he strode towards an arched wooden door marked: *Magistrate. Private.* Rollison watched it close behind him; then, feeling a rising curiosity, glanced round for a newspaper which might help him to understand more about the charge. He was beginning to thirst for knowledge of Madam Melinska and her assistant, Mona Lister.

Nimmo came out, wearing a gown; an M.A. gown.

Almost immediately, Rollison followed him up the steps, past the dock with its shiny brass rail, close to the bench to which Nimmo was climbing. The clerk to the Court had summoned everyone to stand, and a solid mass of people rose. Rollison was close to the dock and expected to be moved on at any moment.

Nimmo sat down; everyone sat down except the mass of people jammed in the doorway. Nimmo glanced across, and said:

"Those who can sit down may stay."

So he was in a genial mood, thought Rollison.

There was much shoving and pushing and whispering; then surprisingly, a hush: and in the hush Nimmo looked down at the clerk, and said:

"I'll take the first case."

"Very good, your honour." The clerk whispered to an usher, the usher whispered to a policeman, by some magic signal the door at the foot of the steps opened, and a wardress appeared; then a girl; next a dark, gipsy-like woman; and finally a second wardress. The clerk was whispering to the magistrate, until quite suddenly formality took over.

"Prisoners in the dock – answer to your names, please. Mona Daphne Lesley Lister."

The girl nodded. Her reply was almost inaudible.

"Madam Melinska."

"I am Madam Melinska," the older woman said.

She had a soft but carrying voice with a faintly foreign inflection; she might be Spanish, Rollison thought, or Italian, or Southern French. She glanced away from the clerk and then saw Rollison – and on that instant Rollison's whole mood changed, from one of lively interest to one of absolute astonishment.

For she looked at him.

And she smiled.

And her lips formed his name with great, almost loving care.

"Mr. Rollison," she said.

Although Rollison heard no sound from her lips and no one else could possibly have heard, there was hushed silence in the Court, and everyone, from Nimmo down to the humblest usher, was staring at the woman.

3

THE CHARGE

It seemed a long time before the silence and the stillness were broken by the magistrate, who shifted back in his carved oak chair and gave a deprecatory, almost apologetic, cough. The clerk to the Court came out of his spell, the men and women jammed tightly in the Press box and the public galleries relaxed and fidgeted. A faint hiss of sound came.

"That's Rollison . . . *Rollison* . . . the *Toff* . . ."

A sturdy, youthful, puzzled chief inspector was approaching the witness-box. The clerk was reading out the charge.

" . . . did conspire together to advise certain persons to buy shares in a company known as Space Age Publishing, Limited, and did misappropriate the money so obtained . . ."

Rollison came out of a kind of coma. "She must have seen a photograph," he muttered aloud. "She's certainly never seen me."

"*Silence!*" called an usher.

"Do the accused plead guilty or not guilty?" inquired Nimmo.

"Not guilty, your honour."

"Not guilty," whispered Mona Lister.

"Are they represented?" demanded Nimmo.

"No, your honour. I understand they wish to apply to the Court for legal aid."

Someone at the back of the Court said clearly: "What a racket! She's as wealthy as sin!"

"If there are any more interruptions I shall have the Court cleared," threatened Nimmo. "Is there any evidence of means?" When neither the woman nor the girl spoke, Nimmo glanced towards the detective about to take the stand: "Can the police give us any information?" The man made no comment. "Very well, we shall hear the evidence of arrest and then consider the application for legal aid."

The inspector took the oath.

" . . . and nothing but the truth, so help me God. On the third day . . . and warned them that anything they said would be taken down and could be used as evidence."

"Did they reply to your charge?" asked Nimmo.

"Yes, sir."

"What did they say?"

"The younger of the accused said it was a frame-up."

"*Indeed.*" Nimmo's voice was like ice.

"Yes, sir. The older of the accused said she didn't understand."

"Did she say *what* she didn't understand, Inspector?"

"No, sir, she appeared to be very puzzled."

"I see. Well, they have been charged and they have

entered a plea of not guilty. Have you the necessary evidence to proceed?"

"No, your honour. We should like to apply for a remand so as to complete our inquiries."

Nimmo's eyebrows rose.

"Bail?" he inquired.

"We have no objection, sir."

"Are there any sureties for the accused in Court?" asked Nimmo. No one replied. There was a sense of tension and of waiting, a look of pleading on the older prisoner's face, and one of defiance on the girl's. All at once Nimmo came to a quick, brusque decision.

"I bind both the accused over in sums of one hundred pounds each. *Are* there sureties?"

The magistrate was leaning forward to the dock.

"*Can you find one hundred pounds each?*" he asked in a clear whisper; and Nimmo, a stickler for the etiquette of the Court, did no more than look his disapproval.

Rollison said very clearly: "I will go surety in those sums, your honour."

Nimmo, Madam Melinska, the girl, everyone else in Court, turned swiftly towards him. Then Madam Melinska smiled once again.

After that, it was simply a matter of formalities, answering questions from the Press and arranging for an eager-to-help woman journalist — Olivia Cordman, Features Editor of *The Day*, to see the two accused women to their home. Rollison suddenly realised that he had no idea where they lived; but doubtless Olivia, who was an old acquaintance, would get in touch with him, if not the women themselves.

At last, he was out of the Court.

At last, he was back at Gresham Terrace.

As his taxi turned in from the end nearest Piccadilly, he saw the small crowd gathered outside Number 22, where he lived. Several were young women, several were middle-aged; there were two or three elderly men as well as a young exquisite in a sapphire-coloured velvet jacket, green, cravat-type tie, and stove-pipe trousers. He had long, silky, beautifully groomed fair hair. As Rollison got out of the taxi, it was this young man who held his attention, and although he was aware of the others he took little notice of them — not even when a small excited cheer rose up.

Rollison paid the taxi-driver, then turned towards Number 22. On closer inspection the young man's face was long, thin, hollow-cheeked; he had dark-fringed lashes over disappointingly small and watery eyes.

Beyond him stood a policeman, there doubtless to clear a path.

A girl shouted: "Good old Toff!"

"You'll be rewarded."

"They didn't mean any harm, Mr. Rollison."

"They —"

In a deep, throbbing voice a woman cried: "They killed my husband. And *I'd* like to kill *you*."

As she spoke, she tossed what looked like a small glass ball towards him, and Rollison had a sudden, blinding fear that it might contain some kind of corrosive acid. He saw the liquid inside it, shimmering in the sunlight, ducked, but could not avoid the missile. It struck his forehead, burst with a sharp "pop!" and liquid began to spill down his face, ice cold, yet burning.

A girl screamed.

The policeman roared: "Hey!"

Sharp pain struck at Rollison's eyes, but even as it did so, panic began to recede; this was ammonia, painful and unpleasant but nothing to cause permanent injury. Yet for the moment he was blinded — and suddenly he was in the middle of a surging furious mob. Above the shouts of anger came a woman's sudden cry of fear, drowned by the policeman's bellow:

"Let her alone!"

Car engines sounded, the screams and shouts merged into a dull roar, someone was sobbing, and all Rollison could see through his tears of pain was a haze of light and surges of colour and movement. Helpless, he stood absolutely still until a familiar voice sounded close by — Jolly's voice.

"Let me pass, please. Let me pass. *Thank* you. Let me pass . . ."

Then Jolly was at Rollison's side.

"Is it —" he began, anxiety roughening his words.

"Ammonia," said Rollison. "What's going on?"

"If you'll come with me, sir —"

"*What's going on?*"

"I'll tell you what's going on," drawled the young man in the velvet jacket. "The little dears are tearing the old darling to pieces. Preserve me, I pray, from the fair sex."

Jolly ignored him. "There's no cause to worry, sir. The police have the situation well in hand."

"I wish to heaven I could see," Rollison said testily.

"Permit me to be your eyes," said the youth, still with the same affected drawl. "Two policemen are now protecting the old darling, and several worthy citizens are grappling with the little dears as if it gives them great pleasure."

"*Please* come indoors, sir," pleaded Jolly.

"Did they attack the woman who threw the ammonia?"

"I think so, sir."

"They did indeed," murmured the young man.

"Perhaps you'd be kind enough to help me upstairs," said Rollison. "Jolly, will you go and find that woman and bring her after us — I'd like to talk to her."

"*Very* well, sir," said Jolly, his voice dull with disapproval. He made his way towards the woman, who was leaning against the railing outside the house, hair awry, an ugly weal on her cheek.

Meanwhile the young man had taken Rollison's elbow and was steering him through the front door of Number 22. Rollison touched the handrail.

"I can manage now, thanks," he said. "Will you lead the way?"

The young man nodded and went ahead, his footsteps sounding clearly on the haircord stair-carpet. Rollison's eyes, still stinging, were nevertheless much better than they had been, and by the time they reached his flat he could even make out the number on the door. Groping in his pocket, he took out a key and held it towards the stranger.

"Will you?"

"My pleasure," the young man said, taking the key.

Once inside the flat, Rollison could find his way blindfold, and he went straight to the bathroom, the young man by his side. He groped for taps; they were turned on for him, the water mixed to tepid warmth. He bathed his face gently, and when he had finished, the young man handed him a towel. Rollison dabbed himself dry, and now found that he could see quite well; most of the pain had gone.

"Thanks," he said gratefully.

"At your service," the young man said. "Feeling more yourself?"

"Much more. Let's go into the living-room."

Rollison led the way, noting how the other's gaze moved swiftly to the Trophy Wall and was held in fascination. He waved his guest to a chair and proffered cigarettes from a carved Malaysian box. The young man selected one with care.

"My name," he said, "is Lucifer Stride."

"Ah," said Rollison. "Lucifer Stride. Were you in Court this morning?"

"I was. Tell me, Mr. Rollison—" the young man leaned forward in his chair—"*do* you think you can help Madam Melinska and Miss Lister?"

Rollison, vision now nearly normal, was watching him intently. His visitor's eyes were sharper than he had thought, rather deep-set and close together. His age was around the middle twenties. By the intensity of his expression, Rollison could see that the asking of this question was the entire purpose of his visit.

"I'll certainly do my best," he answered lightly. "Though I haven't had a chance yet to study the case."

"But Madam Melinska *isn't* guilty, sir, I *know* she isn't. *Nor* Miss Lister," the young man added hastily.

"*How* do you know?" Rollison asked sharply.

The close-set eyes dropped to the floor, evading Rollison's penetrating gaze. "I – er – I —"

The front door bell cut sharply across the stranger's fumbling attempts at explanation.

4

FLAT FULL

Rollison wondered what was going through the young man's mind. Who was he, he wondered, and what was his real interest in the case? Oh well, he would have to find out later.

"Come and see this," he invited.

Followed by the stranger, he went into the hall, and standing a few feet from the door, looked upwards. Over the lintel was a small periscope-type mirror, and this now showed a miniature reflection of Jolly, the woman who had thrown the ammonia, and a policeman.

"Old-fashioned, but effective," remarked Lucifer Stride. This few minutes respite had given him a chance to recover his sang-froid.

"An anachronism," thought Rollison, as he opened the door.

Jolly, standing nearest to him, looked searchingly into his face, was obviously reassured, and immediately relaxed.

"Mrs. Abbott, sir," he said.

The woman looked dazed, and now the weal on her

cheek was much redder and more noticeable. The policeman was holding her arm.

"Come in, Mrs. Abbott," Rollison said, and for once
wished there was another woman in the flat. He led the
way to the living-room. Jolly moved ahead and pushed
a pouffe into position in front of an armchair. Mrs.
Abbott was helped into the chair, only Lucifer standing
aside with real or affected indifference. Jolly disappeared.

The policeman turned to her reassuringly. "Now
don't you worry, you'll be all right now you're with
Mr. Rollison." Anxiously he added to Rollison: "You
don't intend to make a charge, do you, sir?"

"No," Rollison answered.

"Very generous of you, sir. Now if you'll excuse me,
I've a lot to do downstairs."

"What's happening in the street?" asked Rollison.

"Everything's quieter, but we had to arrest three of
the young women, sir."

"I see," said Rollison, glumly. "Was anyone else
hurt?"

"No, sir."

"But don't be surprised if some are," interpolated
Lucifer.

The policeman looked at him, appeared ready to ask
questions, thought better of it and went towards the
door. Rollison saw him out, returning to find Jolly
sponging Mrs. Abbott's forehead, with Lucifer looking
on sardonically. There was now time to study the
woman. She was in her middle fifties, Rollison judged —
her grey hair seemed to be naturally curly, and in a

rather heavy, almost masculine way, she was good-looking. Her eyes were closed, as if she felt relaxed and soothed by Jolly's ministrations.

Jolly drew back.

"A cup of coffee, madam?" he suggested, and without waiting for a reply he disappeared in the direction of the kitchen.

Rollison and Lucifer Stride stood looking at Mrs. Abbott, who kept her eyes closed. After a few moments Stride moved to study the Trophy Wall. Suddenly Mrs. Abbott opened her eyes and looked straight at Rollison. Not long before she had cried in rage: "They killed my husband. And *I'd* like to kill *you*."

Rollison smiled at her.

"Hallo," he said. "Feeling better?"

She didn't answer.

"You look better," Rollison said. "Why did you throw that ammonia at me?"

Still she didn't answer.

"Better still," said Rollison, "who paid you to?"

In a flash, she cried: "No one paid me!"

Lucifer stood with his head tilted back, as if he were trying to see the bullet holes in the crown of the old top hat. The light from the window glinted on his hair, making it look like spun gold. Rollison moved away from the woman, who was staring at him as if in horror and alarm. Jolly came in, with a tray. Rollison did not repeat his questions but turned away,

"I did it because of my husband," Mrs. Abbott cried.

"I'm sorry about your husband," Rollison said gently. "What happened?"

"That devil killed him."

Jolly was pouring out coffee.

"Which devil?" inquired Rollison.

"Madam Melinska!"

"When?"

"It was last year, she —"

"But Madam Melinska only arrived in England a few months ago."

"My husband met her in Rhodesia," said Mrs. Abbott. "She got her talons into him just like she got them into those other poor fools, and persuaded him to give her money. She was going to invest it for him, if you please! I told him not to trust her, but he would do it, and he lost every penny." Her face was twisted, her lips working. "And then he killed himself." She stretched trembling fingers for the cup Jolly held towards her. "And all because of that woman, that — that *bitch*!"

"Or witch?"

Mrs. Abbott caught her breath.

"What do you mean — *witch*?"

"Some people call seers witches."

"*She's* no seer, she just pretends she can look into the future. She doesn't care what lies she tells anyone provided she can get her hands on their money. She —"

The telephone bell rang, and she broke off. Rollison moved towards it and lifted the receiver, thinking more about what Mrs. Abbott had been saying than about the call. Was she speaking the truth, and was Madam Melinska responsible for her husband's death? Or was she lying?

"This is Rollison," he said into the telephone.

"Hallo again, Richard," said Lady Hurst. "I will say that you excelled yourself this morning."

"I'm delighted you approve," said Rollison mildly.

"I approve very much. There is another thing I would like you to do for me, Richard."

"What is it?"

"Bring those two unfortunate women here."

"To the Marigold Club?" Rollison asked, not really surprised.

"Yes. They will be much safer and will certainly be subjected to much less annoyance and publicity," said his aunt. "I have two adjoining rooms ready for them on the second floor. When do you think they can be here?"

"I really don't know, Aunt," Rollison answered. "The Features Editor of *The Day* took pity on them, and I imagine is now offering them a fortune for their story."

"Far more than it's worth, I've no doubt," Lady Hurst prophesied. "But they'll need all the money they can get. Find them, Richard. I would like them *both* here as soon as possible."

"Yes, Aunt," said Rollison meekly, hearing the telephone click as she rang off.

He put the receiver down slowly, aware of Lucifer Stride watching him, of Jolly going back to the kitchen, of Mrs. Abbott having a second cup of coffee. His aunt's voice seemed to echo in his ears; she was right, too. The two women *would* need all the money they could get. And this pointed to a strange, almost bewildering fact. Madam Melinska and Mona Lister had lured thousands to the Court; they were front page news. These were days in which a well-known astrologer could make a very good income indeed from a column in almost any newspaper or magazine.

Why, then, were these two so poor?

He moved across to Mrs. Abbott, who now gave the impression that she was on the defensive; Rollison could not make up his mind whether to bully or to humour her and decided on humouring, at least for the time being.

"Did your husband see Madam Melinska very often?"

"Often *enough*."

"Was she a popular seer?"

"Too popular, if you ask me."

"Did she earn much money?"

"*Earn?* She's never earned a penny. But she's swindled thousands out of the poor devils she's taken in. Don't believe this story about her being poor — she's got a fortune salted away somewhere. You be careful of that woman, Mr. Rollison — she's a snare and a delusion. Any man who falls under *her* spell will find himself penniless when he wakes up to what she really is."

There was venom but also an apparent ring of truth in the words. Rollison moved back — and as he did so, the front door bell rang once again. This time, Lucifer Stride moved towards it, but Rollison went ahead, while Jolly's footsteps were audible as he approached from another passage. So, all three men stood together looking up at the periscope mirror.

There, on the doorstep, were three women.

One was Olivia Cordman of *The Day*; one was Mona Lister; the third was Madam Melinska.

Lucifer made a faint whistling sound and looked at

Rollison, eyebrows raised. Jolly pursed his lips. Before any of them moved the bell rang yet again. Olivia Cordman, small and red-haired and impatient, seldom waited long for anybody.

Rollison said: "I'm going back into the living-room. Make sure that Madam Melinska comes in ahead of the others."

"Very good, sir," said Jolly.

For a few seconds Lucifer Stride appeared to be un-decided as to whether he should stay in the hall or follow Rollison. Then, as Rollison strode forward, he asked:

"May I join you?"

"Yes," said Rollison briskly. He hurried back to the living-room, followed by Lucifer. "Go over by the far window — you can see them both from there."

Lucifer obeyed, moving very soft-footedly, and Rolli-son stood with his back to the fireplace so that he too could see both Mrs. Abbott and the doorway. He re-called the venom in her voice and the way she had tossed the ammonia ball at him. All she could throw this time was the cup and saucer; uneasily, he wished he had taken them away from her. But it was too late now, for Jolly was saying:

"Good afternoon, madam."

"Is Mr. Rollison in?" asked Olivia Cordman.

"Yes, madam, if you will please step this way —"

Jolly manoeuvred so that Madam Melinska came forward first. Rollison tried to glimpse the faces of both women, but he was most anxious to see Mrs. Abbott's. So far, she had no idea who was coming in.

Then Madam Melinska appeared.

Rollison saw her stop short; heard Mrs. Abbott exclaim and saw her spring to her feet. For a moment he was afraid that he had done the wrong thing, that she would attack the other woman; but all she did was to stand by the chair.

Madam Melinska glanced towards her, her face expressionless. Then she saw Rollison, and the smile she gave him was gentle and quite delightful.

"I am very glad to meet you, Mr. Rollison."

Olivia Cordman, obviously puzzled, followed her. She looked at Mrs. Abbott, started to speak, and then thought better of it, obviously thinking it wise to await events.

Then Mona Lister appeared.

Rollison realised on the instant that Mona Lister both knew and feared Mrs. Abbott. He saw her expression of astonishment, the way she stood stock still, hands raised as if ready to fend off an attack. Olivia Cordman's eyes sparked with interest. Lucifer took two long strides forward.

Then Mona cried: *"Don't let her touch me! Keep her away!"* She cowered back against an astonished Jolly.

Mrs. Abbott actually raised the cup, as if to throw it, but Rollison stepped forward swiftly and knocked her arm aside. The cup fell on to the carpet but did not break.

"Take that girl out of here," hissed Mrs. Abbott. "Take her away or I'll choke the life out of her."

She took a step forward, as if to prove that she meant exactly what she said.

5

PROTECTION

Rollison watched with bated breath, keenly aware of the reactions around him: Olivia Cordman's fascinated interest, the calmness of Madam Melinska, the anger of Mrs. Abbott, the fear of Mona Lister.

Of her fear, there was no doubt at all.

"I tell you —" hissed Mrs. Abbott between clenched teeth. She looked about to launch herself forward.

Mona screamed.

Lucifer Stride moved very quickly, stepping between the woman and the girl. He thrust his left arm towards Mrs. Abbott, pushing her back into her chair, then put his right arm protectively round Mona's shoulders.

"Mr. Rollison," he declared, in that affected drawl, "I would have you know that that woman is dangerous."

"If it comes to that, so am I," said Rollison. "If you manhandle anyone else in my flat, I'll run you out by the seat of your pants." He moved forward to Mrs. Abbott, and looked down at her. "What's this? A hate campaign?"

She sat back in the chair, face suffused, eyes glittering.

"Let's have it," demanded Rollison. "You wanted to kill me because I befriended Madam Melinska. What's Mona Lister done to make you want to choke the life out of her?"

The woman glared at the girl, but said nothing.

"Listen to me!" ordered Rollison. "You threw ammonia into my face, you can get a long prison sentence for that kind of crime. Do you want me to charge you?" When she still didn't answer but stared up at him defiantly, Rollison snapped his fingers at Jolly. "Jolly, telephone Scotland Yard, tell Mr. Grice I've changed my mind about making a charge against the woman Abbott. I want —"

Mrs. Abbott gasped: "No! No, please – please don't!"

Rollison spun round on her.

"Why do you hate Mona Lister?" When there was still no answer, he raised his voice: "Jolly!"

"Mr. Rollison," interrupted Madam Melinska, "I think I can tell you. And it is quite understandable."

Rollison said gruffly: "Oh, is it?"

"And I believe you will think so, also," said Madam Melinska. "Mona is Mrs. Abbott's niece. They have been like mother and daughter for many years. After a conflict of loyalty Mona came to me, deserting her aunt. *Can* you be surprised at Mrs. Abbott's bitterness?"

The soft, modulated voice held all of them in a kind of thrall: especially Olivia Cordman. When the older woman stopped, heads turned towards Mrs. Abbott, and it seemed to Rollison that now they felt much as he; sorrow, not anger, for the woman who had lost first a

husband then a niece who was like a daughter, to this
gentle creature.

Rollison asked gently: "Is that the truth, Mrs.
Abbott?"

Mrs. Abbott nodded; and there were tears in her eyes,
tears which seemed to create a relaxed silence until
Lucifer Stride let Mona go, giving her shoulder a re-
assuring pat as he did so. Mona stood for a moment
without speaking. Then she said gruffly:

"She drove me into leaving her."

"Mona, my child —" began Madam Melinska.

"It's no use trying to stop me — and it's no use keeping
on defending everybody," Mona went on with unexpected spirit. "She made life absolutely unbearable,
both for me *and* for Uncle Harry. She — she's so posses-
sive, she thinks she *owns* everybody. And if they do any
little thing she doesn't like she gets into these terrible
rages — *terrible* rages. They frighten me — they even
frightened Uncle Harry. Oh, I'm sorry, Aunt Hester —"
Mona turned towards her aunt — "I don't want to hurt
you, I really don't — but you do know it's true."

She passed a shaking hand over her forehead, and
Rollison could see that she too was close to tears.

"And that was why you went to live with Madam
Melinska?" he asked gently.

The girl looked at him without speaking, and Madam
Melinska answered for her.

"Mr. Rollison, it may help you to know that Mona
has a remarkable natural gift of second sight, or clairvoyance. It was this gift which brought us together. Mrs.
Abbott is still a sceptic where foreknowledge of the future

is concerned. But — "Madam Melinska's mildly amused smile appeared again — "aren't most people? Aren't *you?*"

Rollison felt as if he were at the wrong end of a rapier which pinned him against the wall.

"Yes," he admitted.

"Most Virgoans are," declared Madam Melinska.

"Most Virgo — oh." Rollison had been born late in August and knew his sign of the Zodiac, but this had always been a matter for fun rather than serious consideration. He had a momentary flash of thought: *How* had she known his birth date? Then he told himself that she had only to glance at a *Who's Who* to discover it.

"As a matter of personal interest," put in Lucifer quietly, "what is *my* sign?"

Madam Melinska looked at him very directly. "You are a Gemini, probably born on the cusp. You have the fixity of purpose of all Taureans and the love of movement of Gemini people. I imagine you were born later than your mother had expected."

Rollison, startled by the preciseness of the answer, was astonished by the effect on Lucifer Stride, who now stared open-mouthed at Madam Melinska.

"Is that *true?*" cried Olivia Cordman.

Rollison hung on the answer, but allowed himself to see how the others reacted. Mona still battled with tears, Mrs. Abbott thrust her chin out in a kind of defiance, but her gaze was fixed on Stride.

"How the hell do you do it?" he muttered. "How *can* you know?"

"It's another of her tricks," put in Mrs. Abbott.

"Don't let her fool you – she looks up the information first and then pretends the stars told her. It's all rubbish."

"But *were* you born late?" asked Olivia Cordman.

Lucifer Stride had regained his composure. "I really have no idea," he said shortly. Obviously he was not going to favour one side or the other. "And it's time I went – past time." He nodded to Rollison and moved towards the door. Rollison followed him into the hall and they stood by the front door for a moment, Stride tight-lipped, obviously worried.

"So she *was* right," Rollison said.

"When I was a kid I got tired of being told how long my mother had to wait for me. It's – it's uncanny. And Mona told me —" Stride caught his breath. "There can't be anything in it, can there? No one *can* see into the future or into the past?"

"I shall need a lot of convincing," Rollison said reassuringly.

Stride nodded, opened the door and marched out. Rollison watched him walk down the stairs, his jauntiness gradually returning, but he did not look round from the first half-landing.

As Rollison closed the door, Jolly appeared.

"Did you hear that?" Rollison asked him.

"Yes, sir."

"Is it nonsense?"

"I would prefer to suspend judgment," Jolly said handsomely. "Do you intend to ask Miss Cordman to stay for lunch?"

"No, I'll get rid of her," Rollison said. "I —"

A scream cut across his words making the two men spin round. There was a flurry of footsteps in the living-room, what sounded like a struggle, and confused shouting:

"Let me go . . . *let me go!*"

"Hold her!"

"*Stop him!*"

Rollison had a vision of Mrs. Abbott attacking Mona, but as he burst into the living-room he saw Olivia Cordman holding the struggling girl, Mrs. Abbott gaping, Madam Melinska standing by the window and looking down into the street.

" . . . *Stop him!*" cried Mona, as Rollison appeared. "Don't let him go, they're lying in wait for him! They'll kill him!"

She pulled herself free, darted past Rollison and rushed to the door. Rollison hesitated for a split second before turning and rushing after her. He reached the door first, opened it, and bellowed:

"Stride! Come back!"

Only the echo of his own voice answered him, hollow and unrewarding. Just behind, the girl was sobbing:

"They'll kill him, I know they will!"

Rollison raced down the stairs, alarmed in spite of himself. Reaching the passage, he saw the street door was closed – Lucifer Stride had not lost a second. Rollison sprang towards the door and swung it open – and three things happened almost simultaneously.

A car engine roared with sudden, menacing harshness.

Lucifer Stride, halfway across the street, hesitated

and stood with his hands raised, as if mesmerised, as the car raced towards him.

There were two sharp raps as something smashed on the bonnet and against the windscreen.

Rollison, bounding across the pavement, saw the car swerve, saw a white cloud rising from it. He did not stop moving but grabbed Lucifer and pulled him back to safety. He saw Mona, ashen-faced, staring at Lucifer. Two or three people along the street were standing and gaping as the car narrowly missed a lamp-post, and came to an abrupt halt — then both doors swung open and two men scrambled out and began dabbing frantically at the windscreen. Rollison, springing in pursuit, had just sufficient time to notice they were both tall, both dark-haired, before he kicked against a raised paving stone and went sprawling. He managed to protect his face with his arm but jolted himself badly, and lay for a few seconds, hearing the harsh revving of the car engine and knowing that the men had got away.

He picked himself up, cautiously. Lucifer Stride was leaning against the railings, much as Mrs. Abbott had leaned against them an hour or so earlier; the girl was standing beside him. Then two women and an old man came hurrying up, and Jolly appeared at the street door.

Rollison brushed some dust off his jacket.

"Called the police, Jolly?"

"They are on their way, sir."

"Didn't get the number of that car, did you?" Rollison asked. "Or recognise either of the men?"

"No, sir. I didn't get a clear view at all."

"What hit the windscreen?"

"Two packets of flour, sir," Jolly said.

"Quick work, Jolly." Rollison gripped his man's arm. "But for that they'd have got Stride."

Grabbing the young man and the girl by the elbows, he hustled them into the house. They moved mechanically. As the door closed behind them the girl began to shiver and her lips quivered as words tumbled out:

"It — it — it's *horrible — horrible*! I hate it. I tell you I *hate* it!"

"What do you hate?" asked Rollison sharply.

"I hate *seeing* things!" Mona Lister cried. "I can't help it. I *do* see them and I wish I didn't. I *hate* it!"

"Mr. Rollison," said Lucifer Stride in a shaky voice, "she told me what was going to happen to me, and it *did* happen — exactly the way she said it would."

Rollison could see both incredulity and panic in the watery eyes.

6

THE GIRL WHO COULDN'T HELP SEEING

Rollison followed Lucifer Stride into the living-room. Mrs. Abbott hadn't left her chair, Madam Melinska still stood near the window, Mona Lister was standing staring blankly at the Trophy Wall, while Olivia Cordman was at the telephone, talking very quickly and distinctly.

"Yes, that's right . . . Jolly . . . Yes, but for him the man would have been seriously injured . . . Yes, the police are in the street now . . . What? . . . Oh, she has it, don't make any mistake, she has it, *this* isn't phoney . . . Must go now . . . yes, I'll be in touch."

She rang off, her face glowing with excitement.

"Rolly, you saw what happened. You do know she has it, don't you?"

"Who has what?"

"*Mona* has *second sight.*"

"If only I didn't," cried Mona, spinning round so that her skirt swirled and her hair swung. "I'd give anything not to have it. *Anything!*"

"My dear child," said Madam Melinska, "it is a wonderful gift, and you should cherish it."

"But I hate it, I hate it!"

"And *you* ought to be ashamed of yourself for encouraging it," Mrs. Abbott said bitterly to Madam Melinska.

"You know, Mrs. Abbott, you really must pull yourself together," said Madam Melinska gently. "The child has always had this gift. Trying to crush it out of her can only do harm. Mona, child, you should go and lie down."

"I don't want to lie down!"

Madam Melinska looked at Rollison, without speaking, and he found himself turning to Mona and taking her arm. She did not resist as he led her to the spare bedroom, the door of which stood ajar. The bed had been turned down; Jolly was at his absolute best today, thought Rollison.

"That door leads to a bathroom," he said, pointing. "Try to sleep, Mona — and try not to worry."

"How can I help worrying?" she asked distractedly. "How would you like to be able to foresee horrible things happening to your friends?"

Rollison didn't answer. Her eyes looked so tired that he felt quite sure that she would fall asleep the moment he left her. Closing the door firmly behind him, he rejoined the others; but no sooner had he done so than the front door bell rang yet again. This would be the police, of course, to question Lucifer Stride.

It was.

They asked all the usual questions, and Lucifer told

them exactly what had happened, but made no mention of Mona's prophecy.

"And you've no idea *why* these men should attempt to run you down, Mr. Stride?"

"None whatsoever," said Lucifer, almost superciliously; he had regained a little of his composure.

Rollison and Jolly explained their part in it, Madam Melinska and Olivia Cordman confirmed what they had seen from the window, and twenty minutes later the police left.

"Rolly, my love," said Olivia Cordman as the door shut behind them. "I really must fly, *do* give Lady Hurst my regards and tell her I'll do *every*thing I can." She beamed at Rollison, then turned to Madam Melinska and said almost cooingly: "That *is* understood, isn't it? I do have an option on your story until six o'clock this evening?"

The older woman raised a faintly protesting hand. "You know very well that isn't true," she said gently.

"But you promised —"

"No, Miss Cordman. Mona may have promised, but I don't think she should be held to a promise made under duress. And I *never* accept money for my readings or my interpretations."

"Now do be sensible," urged Olivia Cordman. "You will need money for your defence — *and* for Mona's. You can't go on refusing to accept payment."

"I can and I will," said Madam Melinska.

Olivia paused, obviously at a loss. Rollison wondered if she would try again, but all she did was to shrug, pick up her handbag and gloves, and say goodbye — though

Rollison was quite sure she hadn't really taken no for an answer. As he came back from seeing her off, Mrs. Abbott was saying angrily:

"Who *do* you think you're fooling?"

"The only one being fooled here is you," said Madam Melinska, "and you are fooling yourself." She turned to Rollison. "Mr. Rollison, I cannot thank you enough for your kindness and help, and I do want to assure you of one thing: I have certain gifts which are quite genuine — I am not a charlatan. To prove this to the satisfaction of sceptics, I will accept no money for my readings. And Mona *does* have second sight. She is a natural clairvoyante. In all my years," the woman went on with curious emphasis, "I have never known anyone with the gift developed so highly. Properly guided and encouraged, she will become a very great seer, perhaps the greatest the world has known. It would be wicked to do anything to discourage her."

"It would be wicked to let her go on," said Mrs. Abbott. "It's a lot of mumbo-jumbo, I don't care what you say."

"The car which nearly ran me down was hardly mumbo-jumbo," interpolated Lucifer Stride.

"How do you know *she* didn't arrange it and tell Mona what to say?" Mrs. Abbott rose out of her chair, pointing an accusing finger.

Madam Melinska, still with that strange dignity, looked back at her, calm-faced and serene.

"Hester," she said quietly, "I wish I knew why you hate me so."

"I hate you because you killed my husband, I hate

you because you've stolen my niece, and I hate you because you're a fake!" cried Mrs. Abbott. She turned towards Rollison. "And if *you* help her, *you'll* be as bad! If you've any sense at all you'll send her packing, and then my niece will come back to me."

Madam Melinska shrugged. "Mona is quite free to go back to you whenever she wishes."

"No she isn't! You have some hold over her, you —"

"Aunt Hester," Mona said from the door, "I can't ever come back and live with you. It wouldn't work, really it wouldn't. And neither of us would be happy."

Her aunt swung round. She looked at Mona accusingly, her eyes flashing.

"You—you ungrateful little chit. I wouldn't *have* you back. You've chosen your precious Madam Melinska, and you can have her. But he laughs best who laughs last, my girl, don't you forget that." Gathering up her handbag and gloves with hands quivering with rage and hysteria, she stumbled unsteadily towards the door.

Stride hesitated, and then said under his breath:

"She's not well enough to go on her own."

"She certainly isn't," agreed Rollison. "Will you go with her?"

"Well, *someone* ought to. I suppose it might as well be me." Stride paused for a moment, as if uncertain, then hurried after Mrs. Abbott.

Rollison moved over to the window. In a few moments he saw Mrs. Abbott stumble down the street, saw Lucifer Stride hurry after her and take her arm. On the other side of the road two men were loitering, one big and

burly, the other like a wizened jockey. The jockey turned
in the wake of the couple, and Rollison watched this
with satisfaction. Madam Melinska joined him, saw the
man walking after the others, and spoke with the sharp-
ness of alarm.

"Look at that man!"

"So *you* haven't second sight," Rollison said drily.

"I don't understand you."

"That is a friend," Rollison said. "Jolly must have
telephoned for help." He looked into the woman's
puzzled eyes and felt a strange moment of satisfaction,
for her anxiety somehow made her more human. "His
name is Charlie Wray. He was once a very good light-
weight boxer and he now works at a gymnasium owned
by a friend of mine – Bill Ebbutt. We work together a
great deal."

"Why have you had them followed?" asked Madam
Melinska.

"Not *them*. Stride. There are one or two things I'd
like to know about that young gentleman," said Rollison slowly. He turned away from the window. "And
there are a great number of other questions I'd like
answered," he added. "First and foremost, what *is* all
this about?"

"All I can tell you is that there is a conspiracy to
discredit me and Mona," Madam Melinska told him. "I
don't know why and I don't know by whom, but I *do*
know that you are going to find the answers to both
questions."

"How can you know?" Rollison demanded.

"Because it is in the stars," the woman said, and

touched his arm gently. "You don't have to believe me, Mr. Rollison — but you will find yourself quite unable to resist continuing with this work. I don't think you will ever be convinced of certain things, but I am quite sure you will never reject them absolutely." She paused, and then went on: "And I cannot thank you enough for the help you have already given us."

Rollison said gruffly: "I've done nothing, yet."

"You have helped a great deal," Madam Melinska said, "and will help a great deal more." She paused for a moment, then added gravely: "And unless you're very careful indeed you will be seriously injured while doing so."

Rollison could not keep off the chill which followed her words.

Charlie Wray looked a fool, and often behaved like one. He also looked — at a distance — like a child, and often behaved like one. But he had certain qualities in which he was second to none, and he was probably a better shadow than any expert at Scotland Yard. In middle-age he was almost as fit and tough as he had been at the height of his boxing career, and when following a quarry, as now, he thoroughly enjoyed himself.

Anticipating Rollison's wishes to know more about Lucifer Stride, Jolly had telephoned Charlie Wray, asking him to tail a man who would shortly be leaving Rollison's flat.

Jolly's description had been good, but Stride's appearance still came as a shock to Charlie.

"Man," he muttered to himself as he turned the

corner of Gresham Terrace, "he's about as much a man as my Aunt Emma. Cor lumme, what are they coming to these days. Can't tell boy from girl." Charlie, fond of talking to himself, gave a broad grin as he watched Stride and Mrs. Abbott walking along Piccadilly. "Wonder where they'll go . . ."

They crossed the road by Green Park and reached a bus stop, where there was already a small queue. Charlie held back until a free taxi came along, and hailed it.

"Follow the bus I tell you to," he ordered. "And look out for that blond fellow in the blue jacket, talking to the old girl with grey hair. Let me know if you see them get off."

The cabby, little more than a boy, said "Okay!" with great eagerness.

A bus came along almost at once and the couple boarded it. The cabby followed – through Knightsbridge, then along Brompton Old Road, then into Fulham Road. Charlie sat back, smoking in a lordly fashion. Slowly they lumbered over Stamford Bridge towards Fulham Broadway, and then the driver looked over his shoulder and said excitedly:

"Here they come."

"Drive past," hissed Charlie.

The driver overtook the bus and pulled up in front of a large removal van, which effectively screened it from Stride and Mrs. Abbott. Charlie paid the driver off, and sauntered back along the street until he saw his quarry turn down a side road of shabby terrace houses. By the time Charlie had reached the corner, Mrs. Abbott was standing beneath a shallow porch while Lucifer Stride waited on the pavement.

"Quite sure you're all right?" His words floated back to Charlie.

The woman mumbled her reply.

"Sure you wouldn't like me to come up with you?"

Charlie saw the woman shake her head. Then she disappeared into the house.

He moved into a doorway and waited to see what his quarry would do next—would he carry on down the street, or would he turn back? But for the next twenty minutes or so Stride stood irresolutely outside the house into which his companion had disappeared. Charlie, peering from his doorway, watched him looking anxiously up at the windows. "He's worried about the old girl," thought Charlie. "Can't make up his mind whether he ought to go in after her or not."

But at last Stride came to a decision, and with one last backward look, he retraced his steps towards the main road. Charlie dived back into his doorway, and Stride passed without a glance. Charlie gave a little grin of satisfaction—but as he swung in the wake of his quarry, a sudden clatter of footsteps behind him made him turn his head. Looking back, he saw two tall dark-haired men leap into a small black car which had been parked along the street.

Charlie shrugged. "Some folk are *always* in a hurry," he thought. Then, with a start of dismay, he realised that Stride had reached the main road.

"Gawd!" exclaimed Charlie. "I'll lose him."

He dashed across the road after his quarry—then heard the car close behind. He glanced over his shoulder.

As he did so, he felt a terrible surge of fear, for the car

was heading straight towards him. He made a desperate effort to get clear.

One moment he was running.

The next there was an awful crunch of sound, and his body went sailing through the air.

As it thudded to the ground the car roared up the road and disappeared round a corner.

7

"OLD GLORY"

Rollison turned the wheel of his Bentley into a square of Georgian houses in the middle of which was a beautifully tended garden – a few late flowering shrubs, two magnificent beds of red and pink tulips, and a stretch of bright green lawn enclosed in black iron railings. At one side of the square three houses had been knocked into one, and now comprised the Marigold Club. This had been described by cynics as a house for fallen angels, but in fact it was a club for women in genuine distress, whether the distress was caused by a faithless lover, an errant husband, or some less emotional crisis. Lady Hurst owned it. Lady Hurst had conceived it. Lady Hurst ran it – although with the help of a staff of remarkable efficiency. The manageress, a little, auburn-haired woman with a pleasant face and clear, green-gold eyes, opened the door as the Bentley drew alongside.

No one knew how she managed it, but there was always room to park outside the home of Lady Hurst.

As Rollison stood aside for Madam Melinska and

Mona Lister to enter, she appeared at the foot of the stairs, tall, erect, Victorian in appearance and in severity of manner. Her plentiful near-white hair was swept upwards in Edwardian style, her skirts rustled, rows of pearls on the high neck of her grey silk dress were lustrous and somehow restful.

She came forward, arms outstretched, to greet Madam Melinska.

"My dear, how *very* nice to see you. And Mona, too. Come along in." She turned to Rollison. "You, too, Richard."

It was a command.

"If we can talk business," Rollison said.

"Don't you think that Madam Mel —"

"Aunt," said Rollison firmly, "we're in deep waters and if we're to get out we need to use every minute."

Lady Hurst fingered her horn-rimmed lorgnette.

"Very well," she said, "but I hope you won't be too long."

They were moving towards a high-ceilinged, gracious room with beautifully-carved oak mantel-surround and ceiling of flowers and cherubim. Velvet curtains of pale blue draped the high windows. It was like a scene out of Jane Austen, Rollison reflected.

"Well, Richard," his aunt said when they were settled.

"The police don't bring a charge like this without some cause," Rollison declared. "I haven't studied the circumstances yet, but you seem to be convinced of Madam Melinska's integrity. Why, then, did the police bring this charge?"

Mona clenched her hands in her lap. Madam Melinska smiled faintly.

Lady Hurst looked almost fearsome. "I was and am quite assured of good faith."

"The charge says that Madam Melinska and Mona conspired together —"

"They did *not* conspire."

"But Madam Melinska advised you to buy shares in Space Age Publishing, did she not? And now, not only has the money you invested disappeared, but the company is virtually insolvent."

"It was not insolvent at the time she advised me to invest," Lady Hurst stated, "was it, Madam Melinska?"

The way she asked that question seemed to suggest that a simple "no" would be sufficient to satisfy her nephew, if not the law. Madam Melinska, hands resting on the arms of her chair, shook her head.

"Not to my knowledge," she said.

"*Did* you advise people to buy them?"

"I don't know," said Madam Melinska quietly.

"*You don't know?* You mean you don't remember?"

"I do not recollect what I say when advice is being given through me. I am simply the channel through which the advice is given."

"You mean you are in a trance?" Rollison asked faintly.

"Richard," cautioned his aunt warningly. "Don't sneer."

"The last thing I'd do, Aunt. The very last thing. But were *you* advised by Madam Melinska when she was in a trance?"

"Yes."

"And you *took* her advice?"

"Yes."

"Goodness gracious," Rollison said, in hollow tones. "Did Madam Melinska tell you that these shares were a good investment?"

"She did."

"Did you pay *her* the money?"

"I sent a cheque to the company, but they say they never received it. The cheque was cashed and endorsed on behalf of the company but the police say it didn't go through the company's books."

"Well, it might help if we knew who cashed it," said Rollison drily. "Have any of you any idea?"

"None at all," said Madam Melinska. "None at all, Mr. Rollison."

"*That* is what you are to find out," added Lady Hurst, severely.

Rollison frowned. "I'm sorry, Aunt. The whole thing sounds a complete cock-and-bull story, and that's what the police think it is. The company was —"

"The company was, and should still be, a perfectly reliable one," Lady Hurst said. "It has been established for over sixty years and *I* have known of it for most of that period. It was and should still be flourishing."

Rollison looked thoughtful.

Before bringing Madam Melinska and Mona Lister to the Marigold Club, he had been busy telephoning newspaper friends as well as friends in the City, and he now knew most of the story. Space Age Publishing, Limited had once, as his aunt said, been a flourishing company.

Then, quite recently it had been sold, and within a few months ugly rumours of bad debts, unpaid accounts and serious shortages in stocks began to circulate. It was now known that the company was virtually bankrupt.

"What went wrong doesn't necessarily concern us," said Rollison. "Nevertheless, this was the company in which Madam Melinska persuaded you, and others, to invest. Where did the money for those investments go? As I said, it appears to have completely disappeared – and it seems that the police think Madam Melinska and Mona have something to do with its disappearance."

"The charge is absurd," said Lady Hurst. "Why, neither of them could even pay for their own bail."

Rollison frowned. "Some people think that this is a sham – that Madam Melinska has the money but is pretending poverty in order to *make* the charge seem absurd."

"Do *you* believe that, Mr. Rollison?" asked Madam Melinska quietly.

Rollison looked at her without speaking, feeling an odd compulsion to say: "No." But until there was proof of what had happened to the missing money, no one could be sure.

The dark, compelling eyes met his.

"If you help to find the truth you may be badly hurt, Mr. Rollison, many of your friends may turn against you. But you will get help from unexpected sources."

Rollison stared back, determined that her gaze should drop before his; but it did not. He was beginning to wonder how long he could keep this up, to wish that his aunt would make some kind of interruption, when there was a tap at the door.

It was the auburn-haired manageress.

"I'm sorry, Lady Hurst, but there is a telephone call for Mr. Rollison. A Mr. Jolly. He says that it is extremely urgent."

For Jolly to say that, it must be, thought Rollison.

There was no telephone in the drawing-room, and he got up, murmured an apology, and went out. He could feel the gaze of the three women, his aunt's tinged with a slight hostility, Madam Melinska's reproachful, the girl's frightened. He picked up a telephone in the hall.

"Yes, Jolly?"

Jolly said: "It's grave news, sir, I'm afraid." His pause underlined the statement, and Rollison caught his breath in sudden alarm. "Charlie Wray has been fatally injured – in a car accident, so-called. The car didn't stop, but a passer-by took a description of it – and the police think it may well have been the car that tried to run down Lucifer Stride."

From that moment, Rollison's attitude towards the inquiry changed. Until then he had been involved almost in spite of himself. Now, he was involved because he meant to find out who had killed Charlie Wray.

The next few hours were a nightmare.

First, he went to Fulham, to see and identify the body.

Next, he drove to the East End, where Bill Ebbutt lived, massive, flabby, wheezy, generous Bill Ebbutt, who found "work" for a dozen boxing has-beens at his gymnasium which was next to his pub, The Blue Dog,

near the Mile End Road. As the Bentley turned the corner into the mean street of tiny terrace houses, men and
women turned to stare and the whispers began.

"It's the Toff . . . Toff . . . Toff . . ."

"The Toff's here . . ."

Toff, Toff, Toff, Toff . . . Rollison felt that he could
hear the soubriquet from a hundred lips. And he saw
the men and women, brought by the bad news, gathered
outside the wooden gymnasium. The entrance was lined
with people, nearly all of them men — mostly friends of
the dead Charlie, old sparring partners, old opponents
of the ring.

Rollison slammed the door of the car and walked
what seemed an unending gauntlet of sad and familiar
faces. He had asked for help and it had been given
cheerfully; and now one of their friends was dead.

The sun shone out of a clear blue sky. It shone on the
open door of the gymnasium, and then on Bill Ebbutt,
as he appeared, wearing a black polo-neck sweater and
black trousers — as if he were in mourning. The clothes
showed up the pallor of his face.

His big hand engulfed Rollison's.

"Bill," Rollison said, "I couldn't be more sorry."

"I know, Mr. Ar," said Ebbutt, hoarsely. "Helluva
thing to happen. Any idea who did it?"

"Not yet."

"Every mother's son of us will help."

"I know," said Rollison. "As soon as I need help, I'll
tell you. Does Mrs. Wray know?"

"Yeh." Ebbutt gulped. "I told her."

"Is she at home?"

"Yeh."

"Come with me, Bill, will you?"

The little home in a narrow street of old grey hovels soon to be demolished was within walking distance. A dozen silent men followed Rollison and Ebbutt round half a dozen corners and then to a front door painted bright yellow – painted, quite recently, by Charlie Wray. Two or three neighbours were in the tiny front parlour which opened on to the street; they stood aside for Rollison and Ebbutt to enter.

Wray's widow was small and slim, with hair which was still jet black despite her sixty-odd years. She stared at Rollison, her eyes red and swollen, her face streaked with tears.

"Get out of my house," she said. "Don't ever come here again."

"Daisy —" Rollison began.

"Don't speak to me. *Don't speak to me.* If it wasn't for you, he'd be alive. You killed him."

"Now, Dais —" began Bill Ebbutt, in distress.

The woman ignored him, her eyes boring into Rollison with frightening intensity. "Get out of my house. *Get out of my house*, Mr. Rollison. And remember – don't ever come back."

"You may be badly hurt, Mr. Rollison, many of your friends may turn against you . . ."

"Daisy," Rollison said, very quietly, "if I were in your place I would feel exactly as you do. I'm desperately sorry."

He turned and walked into a street which was now crowded. Many of the faces he saw were those of strangers, although there were some he knew, mostly from Bill Ebbutt's gymnasium. A little grey-haired woman, struggling to see over the shoulders of those in front of her, shook her fist.

"You as good as killed poor Charlie!" she called out. "You sent him to his death!"

Uneasily, a man said: "Shut up, Ma."

"I'll shut up when you've shut *him* up."

Ebbutt glared at her.

Rollison gripped his arm. "It's all right, Bill."

But it wasn't all right. The silence was too noticeable, the coolness much too marked, as he walked away. There was hatred in his heart for Charlie Wray's killers, and dismay at the attitude of the people here, so many of them his former friends.

"It's crazy, Mr. Ar," Ebbutt said, "but the talk started even before you got here. They started to say you should have done the job yourself, not got someone else to do your dirty work. I—*hey*! I didn't mean that the way it sounded, I meant . . ."

Bill Ebbutt floundered.

Rollison put a hand on his arm and said: "Don't worry, Bill."

He got into the Bentley and drove away, half expecting something to be thrown at the car; but nothing was thrown. The people just stared blankly and the last he saw of them was a miniature of set, troubled faces in the driving mirror. He turned into the Mile End Road and the roar and throb of traffic. Before he reached the tall spire of Whitechapel Church he knew that this was going to be a case that only he should handle.

Or he and Jolly should handle. He must telephone Jolly.

"The body was found only fifty yards from the house where Mrs. Abbott lives," said Jolly. "Do you think you should go and see her?"

"Yes," said Rollison crisply. "What about Lucifer Stride?"

"He seems to have vanished," Jolly said, glumly. He paused for a moment, and then added: "There *is* one other thing, sir. Have you seen the evening newspaper?"

"No."

"It has a full report of the hearing, and of your generous gesture, sir. As a result there are a great number of people gathered outside, showing very considerable enthusiasm. You might well be advised to come in by the fire escape."

"Oh," said Rollison, taken by surprise. "I'll think about that. Do I hear the other telephone bell ringing?"

"Incessantly, sir," said Jolly. "Incessantly."

When Rollison put the telephone down it was with unexpected lightness of heart. And he seemed to hear a gentle voice saying: " . . . *but you will get help from unexpected sources.*"

8

HOME OF THE ANGRY WOMAN

No one was near 12 Tillson Street, the street in which
Charlie Wray had died. On the roadway and the pavement close to a cracked and broken lamp-post was a tell-
tale patch of fresh sand and dampness from the water
used to hose away the signs of death. It was a short
street, shaped like a shallow crescent between two
longer ones. The houses were all three storeys high, with
steps leading down to gloomy-looking basements; there
were bars at the basement and ground-floor windows of
Number 12, and black paint on the bars and the rail
about the house. In the middle of the basement area
was a large bowl of dead and dying tulips; otherwise the
place seemed well-kept. It was flanked on either side by
FOR SALE boards outside houses much more dilapidated.

Rollison stepped to the front door, and glanced behind him. There was no one in sight—only a small black
car parked fifty yards or so along the road.

On the side of the door were four bells, and beneath
each bell-push a name. The third one from the bottom
had: "*Mrs. Abbott*" in faded ink on a dirty white card.

He pressed Mrs. Abbott's bell, and waited. There was

no answer. He pressed again with the same result. He did not know why he was surprised, but he was; and uneasiness merged into his surprise. He inspected the lock; it was easy to force, and he did not lose a moment. The blade of a special knife, a few dexterous twists – and the latch clicked back. Rollison pushed the door open and stepped inside.

At once he detected a strong smell of burning.

Burning?

He saw stairs disappearing downwards into a well of darkness; more stairs leading up, the walls drab with faded paper. It was from these that the smell of burning seemed to be coming. He hurried upwards, passed a doorway marked 2, and reached the next landing. Beneath the 3 on the door now facing him was the name *Mrs. Abbott*. This door had an old-fashioned type lock, no more difficult to force than that on the main entrance. The smell of fire was much stronger now, and Rollison worked quickly. Suddenly the lock clicked back, and he flung the door open.

Smoke filled a room almost straight ahead, along a narrow passage. It was red-tinged. Rollison coughed as he plunged inside; he could see flames through the swirling grey, but little else. In one corner of the room he could just make out a wash-basin and a large old-fashioned jug. Coughing and choking, he fumbled for a tap, filled the jug, and splashed water over the fire. It seemed an age before the flames went out. He refilled the bowl and splashed in greater volume, this time until there was only smoke and steam and blackened debris.

The window was closed and smoke still whirled and

twisted, as if anxious to get out. Rollison pushed open the window and turned back.

Gradually the smoke cleared; and as it cleared, his smarting eyes made out the hazy shapes of furniture: a chair, a cupboard, then a bed. And lying across the bed, feet dangling to the floor, a woman's body.

Rollison's heart lurched; then he steeled himself to go forward. It was a shock, even though he had been half prepared for some such thing. The woman did not move. Rollison reached her, saw the slackness of her eyes and mouth and knew that she was dead. He leaned forward and looked down on the now flabby face of Mrs. Abbott.

Two had died . . .

The smoke had almost gone, and glancing into a corner he saw a bureau, flap down, drawers wide open. He went over to it. Someone had rifled it, papers were strewn about and two drawers had been turned upside down on the floor. But there was nothing to show what the thief – if thief it had been – had been seeking.

Rollison turned back and studied the position of the dead woman.

If she had come in, *crept* in, and approached a thief from behind, and the thief had heard, he could have spun round, seized her, and easily have thrown her into the position in which she now lay. One shoe had fallen between the bureau and the white bedspread, the other dangled from her foot. Seeing these, Rollison felt sure that this was what had happened.

There were dark marks on Mrs. Abbott's throat, showing where thumbs and fingers had pressed – marks which told how deeply they must have embedded themselves in the thick flesh. No one could kill like this by accident. In fury, perhaps, but chiefly in cold-blooded determination. And the killer must have had powerful hands.

Turning away from the body, Rollison studied a photograph of an elderly man — almost certainly Mrs. Abbott's husband, he thought. Then he made a careful search through the rest of the flat. But he found nothing of interest. And there was no ammonia, nothing to suggest that it was Mrs. Abbott who had made the missile she had thrown at him.

Such missiles couldn't be bought; she must either have made it herself or had it made for her, and Rollison's suspicions that someone had put her up to the attack strengthened. He lingered for a few moments, wondering whether he had overlooked anything, decided not to stay, and went to the front door. There was no telephone, but he could ring the Divisional police from the nearest booth.

He opened the door — and saw two heavily built men standing outside.

Rollison stood stock still in surprise.

The two men blocked his way to the stairs; obviously they intended to do this. He felt quite sure who they were, and almost at once, one of them said:

"Mr. Rollison?"

"Yes."

"We are police officers."

"I was about to telephone Division," Rollison said.

"Were you, sir?" Scepticism showed in the man's voice. "You don't live here, sir, do you?"

"No. You know very well that I don't."

"Just making sure, sir. Excuse me." He pushed by, and as he did so two more men appeared at the foot of the stairs. There would have been no point in trying to get away, but even had he wished to make the attempt, these additional men made any chance of escape almost impossible. Rollison still hadn't fully recovered from his surprise at their unexpected arrival on the scene; now he tried to regain control of the situation.

"Officer."

The man who had pushed past him paused. "Yes?"

"A woman has been killed in this house."

"Indeed, sir. Is that why you were about to call us?"

"Yes."

"What are you doing here?" The second man spoke, the taller and more massive of the two; he reminded Rollison of Bill Ebbutt fifteen years or so ago.

"I came to talk to the woman – to Mrs. Abbott."

"I see, sir."

The first man was walking down the passage. The acrid fumes of smoke were still strong, and Rollison saw him pause and rub his eyes. He turned.

"It looks as if someone decided to burn the place down."

"*What's* that?" Another man appeared on the stairs, youthful-looking and very eager, obviously not a policeman. "Arson, do you mean?" His eyes gleamed with excitement. "I'm from the *Chronicle*. *Is* it arson?"

"Who knows?" asked the policeman nearest Rollison.

"Don't waste any time here, Tommy. Mrs. Abbott's dead, and there was a fire."

The boy's eyes seemed to grow enormous.

"Was she *murdered*?" He looked at Rollison. "Do you know? Are you—good Lord! It's the Toff!"

"That's what they call him," the detective said drily.

"Did *he* find the body?"

"Yes," Rollison answered quickly.

"And *we* found *him*," said the detective.

There was deep hostility in his manner, which was hard for Rollison to understand. It was almost as if the man intended to make the newspaper-man suspect him.

"There'll be a statement later," the detective went on. "That's enough for now."

"But—Mr. Rollison! Haven't *you* a statement to make?"

Rollison clutched at the remnants of his composure, and said firmly:

"Yes, I came here and found her dead."

"So you didn't —" The youth checked himself from finishing "you didn't do it." At any other time Rollison would have laughed, but now, still barely recovered from the initial shock of discovering the dead woman, and from his astonishment at the police attitude, he could see nothing funny in the situation in which he found himself. The newspaper-man gave him one last lingering almost incredulous look, then turned and hurried down the stairs as a police photographer hurried up them. Rollison had the strong impression that the police had been prepared to carry out a murder investigation. He lit a cigarette as he turned back into the flat.

"Where are you going?" demanded the policeman with him.

"Into the sitting-room."

"I'd like you to stay here."

"Why don't you come with me?" asked Rollison. He turned away, expecting a hand to drop heavily on to his shoulder, but the man didn't stop him. The photographer was on the bedroom threshold, where the man who had first spoken to Rollison was saying:

" . . . could have been started to burn the body and disguise the way the woman was killed."

"Who put the fire out?" asked the photographer.

"Good question," Rollison said. He turned to the detective. "Are you in charge?"

"Yes, I'm Detective Inspector Godley."

"*Godley?*"

"That's right."

The obnoxious solicitor at the West London Police Court had been named Godley, also.

"Well, well," Rollison said. "Inspector, it's time I went home."

"I'll tell you when you're free to go, sir."

Rollison said quietly, "I am free to go now."

"No, sir, you're not."

"If you want to prefer a charge I want a lawyer. At once. If you're not going to prefer a charge, I intend to leave. At once."

The man had very steady, rather opaque brown eyes. He had a strong face and a powerful physique, and something about the set of his lips told Rollison he was extremely stubborn. Inside the bedroom, the camera was clicking and men were moving about. A car drew up in the street below.

Rollison said: "I'll be at home when you want me." He tapped the ash from his cigarette, and walked back along the passage. Again he expected to be stopped, but was not. The man should at least have asked him to make a statement.

He reached the door.

"Mr. Rollison?" the man called.

"Yes."

"I would like a statement from you about what happened here."

"I don't know what happened before I came," Rollison said. "I arrived at about four-thirty. I smelled burning, so I broke in. I found a fire in the bedroom, and put it out. As soon as the smoke cleared I saw the woman on the bed. She appeared to have been strangled. I was about to leave and telephone you —"

The man interrupted: "Why not telephone from here?"

"Because there's no telephone."

"Oh." That was the first time the man looked disconcerted, but he quickly recovered. "We shall want your statement in writing, duly signed."

"Whenever you like."

"As it's a short one, why not now, sir?"

Rollison thought: "Yes, why not now? It won't take ten minutes." He went to the sitting-room, and Godley followed, put a pen and a notebook on a table, and left him; but there was another man in the room, watching. Damn it, they *couldn't* seriously believe that he had murdered Mrs. Abbott!

He finished and signed the statement, and took it to Godley, who was back in the bedroom doorway. Godley nodded curtly, and said: "Thank you." Rollison went down the stairs as a short, plump man came up them, a Dr. Sampson, whom he knew as a police-surgeon. Sampson nodded; and passed. Rollison stepped into the street. Outside the house were three police cars, the doctor's car, an ambulance and a crowd of fifty or sixty people. Someone took a photograph – probably a Press photographer. A child asked in a piping voice:

"Did *he* do it, Mummy?"

"Hush!"

Rollison forced a smile. "No, I didn't do it, sonny."

No one spoke to him as he turned towards Fulham Road, where he had left the Bentley. He turned the corner, saw the car, and then noticed someone sitting in the front passenger seat.

It was a woman.

He opened the door, and Olivia Cordman smiled up at him.

"Didn't they arrest you, Rolly?" she asked.

9

WARNING

Rollison went round to the other side of the Bentley, got in, started the engine, and eased off the brake. The car began to move forward. He waited for several cars to pass, then pulled out.

"Can I drop you somewhere?" he asked politely.

"Anywhere near Fleet Street," Olivia said. "Don't look so grim, Rolly. They *didn't* arrest you, did they?"

"They could yet!"

"The great Toff? Don't be silly."

"What brought you here?" asked Rollison, sharply.

"I came to see Mrs. Abbott. I thought if I spoke to her alone, I might discover something that might help Madam Melinska. When I arrived I saw the crowds and someone told me Mrs. Abbott was dead. Then I saw your car – it was unlocked, so I got in – and here I am." Olivia settled more comfortably in her seat.

Rollison smiled. He was only just beginning to thaw out from the chill ice of Godley's manner, and still hadn't quite decided what to do.

"Need a friend?" asked Olivia.

"Now as always."

"Try me. I can be a good one."

"Certainly not," Rollison said. "I'm sure you'd see me get a life sentence if you thought it would put *The Day*'s circulation up."

"You couldn't be more wrong," said Olivia Cordman. "I would only see you get a life sentence if –" she paused, rolling the words on her tongue, and gave him a bright, friendly smile – "if I thought you'd killed Hester Abbott."

"Do you?"

"Well, she *did* threaten you, didn't she."

"So she did," agreed Rollison.

"And no one in their right mind is going to believe it was simply because you were helping Madam Melinska – even though she *was* supposed to have driven her husband to his death."

"I see," Rollison said. "That's the angle, is it? Very interesting indeed, Olivia. You don't have to believe me, but I didn't know the first thing about this business until this morning."

Olivia Cordman's grin was quite remarkably disbelieving.

"You're right, Rolly dear – I *don't* have to believe you. Neither does anyone else."

Rollison felt a flare of exasperation, but quickly stifled it, and laughed at her. The laugh did him good and obviously surprised Olivia, who raised her eyebrows as she turned to look at him. She had beautiful eyes, and Rollison was surprised that he hadn't noticed them before.

"If you're to be a friend," he said, "you have to believe me."

"Then why not try telling me the truth." She was still piqued by his laughter.

Rollison suppressed a smile.

"I'll tell you the truth as soon as I know it," he said. "Meanwhile, *you* tell *me* something. You wouldn't be so anxious to get the Melinska story unless it would help your magazine's circulation. Why should it make new readers for *The Day*?"

"My dear," Olivia said, "where *have* you been?"

"There's no need to be so cryptic."

"In the past year or so, Rolly my love, public interest in fortune-telling has multiplied ten times over. When I first became Features Editor of *The Day* the Board wouldn't have a breath of such fantasy. When I suggested it, I was pooh-poohed. Superstitious, sentimental nonsense, the wise men said, not fit for nor wanted by the sturdy housewives of the middle income group who read *The Day*. Whereas now we run a two-page spread every fortnight—we're fortnightly now, in case you don't know."

"I do know," Rollison said, and asked casually: "Think there's something in it?"

Olivia stared at him for a moment, open-mouthed. "Something in it! Something *in* it! My dear Rolly, of *course* there's something in it. Madam Melinska's one of the most *gifted* seers —" She paused, as if at a loss for words.

Rollison chuckled. "Okay, so *you* believe in it. But that —"

Olivia interrupted him. "There *aren't* any 'buts'. I certainly do believe in it, *and* I believe in Madam Melinska, and so do three-quarters of our readers. And if Madam Melinska would sell us her story it would add twenty thousand to our circulation. Can you help us to get it, Rolly?"

Thoughtfully, Rollison said:

"I doubt if anyone will ever make her do anything she doesn't want to do, but *if* she decides to sell, and *if* you'll meet the competition, I'll put in a word for you." He swerved to avoid an oncoming car. "What do you know about Mona Lister?"

"Only that she's been working with Madam Melinska — and that she's a natural born clairvoyante. Why, you saw for yourself how she 'saw' what was going to happen to Lucifer Stride."

"So I did, so I did," murmured Rollison. "Just one more question. What do you know about Space Age Publishing?"

Olivia looked indignant. "I just can't believe that Madam Melinska was involved in anything dishonest," she said flatly. "And if she really *did* advise people to buy shares — well, it *must* have been advice given in good faith. As for Space Age, all I know is that the company changed hands recently and seemed to be doing well. They were planning a very big advertising campaign — money no object — then, suddenly: Phut!" — Olivia snapped her fingers — "they were broke. We were doing some of the advertising for them, and I met the senior partner — Michael Fraser, I think his name was. He had an office in Fleet Street, why don't you go and see him – if he's still there," she added.

Rollison looked thoughtful. "Do you know, Olivia, I think I will." He pressed his foot down on the accelerator, and the big car sped past the Tate Gallery and soon approached the Gothic magnificence of the Houses of Parliament, superb in the early evening sun. Rollison rounded Parliament Square, then went along the Embankment; spotting a parking space near Waterloo Bridge, he pulled in. As he was putting sixpences into the meter, Olivia was flagging down a taxi.

"This time I'll drop you," she said.

The Space Age Publishing offices were in a large new office block within a stone's throw of the Church of St. Clements; Olivia dropped Rollison outside, giving him a searching look from her bright eyes as she waved a nonchalant hand. It was nearly six o'clock and Rollison wondered whether anyone would be in the office. The lift attendant said dolefully:

"Usually go by five-thirty sharp, sir."

As he walked along a bright new passage in the bright new building, a door ahead of him opened and a girl came out. At first, she simply glanced at him – but suddenly, ten feet or so away, her eyes widened, she stared and missed a step. Then she spun round, ran back along the passage, and rushed into the doorway from which she had just come. The door slammed.

Rollison reached the door. On it, in gilt letters, were the words: *Space Age Publishing, Ltd. Mr. Michael Fraser.* Inside the room the girl was talking in a low-pitched voice, conveying the same sense of urgency that her manner had done. Rollison turned the handle and pushed. As the door opened, the girl was saying:

"It *can't* be a coincidence, I'm *sure* it's him!"

Rollison pushed the door wider open. The girl, standing by another open door at the far side of the room, jumped wildly. A man standing in that doorway stared at Rollison in mingled surprise and alarm. He was not Lucifer Stride, but he was remarkably like him, except that his fair hair was short and he was dressed in a well-cut, conventional dark grey suit.

"Good evening," said Rollison. "I gather you're expecting me."

The man drew a deep breath.

"Sooner or later, I suppose we were," he admitted. "It's all right, Jane, you worry too much." He gave Rollison a rather subdued smile. "I suppose you want to know all we can tell you about Space Age Publishing."

"That's exactly what I do want," Rollison agreed.

"You'd better come in," said the man. His likeness to Lucifer Stride was quite remarkable, thought Rollison. "And you'd better come and take some notes, Jane – or better still, fix the tape-recorder so that we've a record of the conversation." He pushed the door behind him wider and stood aside for Rollison to pass.

There was just one thing wrong: the girl's manner.

The man was completely convincing, smooth, pleasant-voiced, but the girl was still agitated. Rollison went forward as if with no suspicions, but at the last moment gripped the man's shoulders, spun him round, and thrust him into the inner room. As he did so, he saw a raised hand flash down from the other side of the door – a hand holding some kind of weapon.

There was a dull, heavy thud.

The man went down like a sack as Rollison, using all his strength, banged the door back against his would-be assailant, pulled it away, then banged it back again. There was a gasp, a groan, the weapon dropped and slithered along the carpet, and the man whom Rollison had squeezed between the door and wall joined his companion on the floor.

Behind Rollison the girl stood, terrified.

Rollison turned and passed her, scarcely out of breath, and twisted the key in the lock of the passage door.

10

BIG DEAL

The girl was slim, delicate-looking, with honey-coloured shoulder-length hair and a fringe. She watched Rollison tensely, following every move he made. When he took her arm, she jumped wildly.

"No need to worry, my dear, just do exactly what I tell you and you'll come to no harm," Rollison promised. "But do it quickly. Go into that room, prop the door wide open—we don't want any *more* people hiding behind it, do we?—then straighten out the joker who knocked the wrong man over the head."

He thought she would be too frightened to obey, but she freed herself and went into the inner room, while Rollison glanced round the outer one. The furniture was plain and spindly; on the walls were drawings, obviously the original artwork for advertisements in newspapers or such magazines as *The Day*. There were two shelves full of books and two filing cabinets as well as three desks, two typewriters, a very small telephone exchange and four telephones.

Jane was blocking the door open with a chair.

The man who had welcomed Rollison so pleasantly

was beginning to stir. Rollison crossed to him, bent down, gripped his coat lapels and heaved him to his feet. Then he half pushed, half lifted him across the inner office. This was a larger room than the other, but furnished in much the same way. Behind a big flat desk, black-topped on auburn-coloured wood, was a swivel desk chair. Rollison moved this with his foot and dumped the man in a sitting position on the floor behind it, his back against the wall. "Don't move," he said shortly, "or I'll call for the police."

The man looked up at him from dazed eyes – but he might not be so dazed as he pretended, reflected Rolli-son, keeping a careful eye on both him and his assailant, who, with the girl's help, was now sitting up. Rollison waited until he was on his feet, and then said:

"And after telephoning the police I'll break your neck. Go and sit next to your friend. On the floor."

The man's hair was ruffled, his tie askew. He was broad-shouldered, solid-looking, and appeared to be in his middle thirties. He began to speak, then changed his mind and did what he was told.

"You, too," Rollison told the girl.

"But —"

"Do I have to make you?"

Meekly, she went to the wall and sat down beside the two men, while Rollison tried to decide the best way to handle the situation. An appearance of omniscience might make the men crack earlier than they would other-wise, but he wasn't sure. Despite what had just hap-pened, neither looked the type to use violence.

Or to do murder.

On the desk was a sheaf of papers protruding from a manilla folder which was tied round with a piece of pink tape. Until then, Rollison had shown no interest in it; now he moved towards it. The man like Lucifer Stride drew in a sharp, hissing breath. Rollison glanced at the folder and read a name, upside down: *Abbott. H. J.* His heart began to beat faster. These papers might have been taken from Mrs. Abbott's flat; if they had, then these men were obviously suspects for the murder. He turned the folder round and pulled the tape; the bow which secured it undid easily.

"Who killed Mrs. Abbott?" he asked casually.

The man like Lucifer Stride gasped.

"*Killed!*" Jane echoed hoarsely.

"Someone choked the life out of her."

"Oh, no!" Jane gasped. "Oh, *no*!"

The broad-shouldered man said breathlessly: "But I never saw her. The flat was empty. She wasn't there."

"My God," said the other man, turning towards him, "if you killed her —"

"I swear I didn't!"

"She can't be *dead*!" cried Jane.

"The police are looking for her murderer," Rollison said. "Or her murderers. And when they discover that you stole these papers from her bureau they'll put two and two together, won't they?" He spread the papers out. There were statements of accounts, share certificates, bank statements, some snapshots of the man whose photograph had been at the flat, one of Mrs. Abbott, one of Mona Lister. Rollison moved back a pace, seeing that the broad-shouldered man was bracing himself, pos-

sibly in an attempt to spring up at him. But he appeared
to notice nothing.

"Where are they?" he demanded.

"Where — where's what?" That was the man who re-
sembled Lucifer Stride. This must be Michael Fraser,
reflected Rollison.

"I don't know what you know about me, Fraser," he
said, "but it doesn't seem enough. You are all three involved in a theft at Mrs. Abbott's flat and you could be
charged with murder. And I'm impatient." After a
pause, he went on harshly: "I'm not here to find out who
killed Mrs. Abbott. That's a job for the police. I am
here to get the papers which were in this file and which
you've taken out. Where are they?" A shot in the
dark, he reflected to himself, but one which might well
find its mark.

It did.

Michael Fraser swallowed. "If we give them to you,
will —"

"Shut up!" rasped the other man.

Rollison stretched a hand towards the telephone. At
this stage he had no intention of dialling Scotland Yard,
but there was no way his prisoners could be sure of that.
He actually put the instrument to his ear and dialled 2
before Jane cried out:

"Don't let him!"

Fraser said chokily: "They're in my brief-case."

"You damned fool," muttered the other. "He
wouldn't call the police. He's bluffing."

Rollison looked at him with raised eyebrows. "I can
assure you, my friend, that I'm not." He picked up the

brief-case, which was black and very heavy. He hadn't the faintest idea what papers it contained, other than that they had been taken from Mrs. Abbott's folder, but did not mean to find out while he was here. "One more thing: why did you suddenly stop your advertising campaign for Space Age Publishing?"

Fraser muttered: "We couldn't pay for it."

"We spent far more than we could afford on layout and artwork," the other man said. "It was a gamble, but we hoped it would pay off. Then that infernal fortune-teller decided to use our name to swindle money out of her fool clients. *We* didn't know anything about it, but mud sticks, and the public will never believe we didn't. Oh well —" he shrugged — "I guess we'll be lucky if we can hold out for another month — that's what that damned fortune-teller did to us."

"Mr. Rollison," Fraser said, "what's your interest in defending this woman?"

"Her reputation," answered Rollison.

"*That* bitch! You don't give a damn for her reputation!"

"As a matter of fact I do," Rollison said, "and in the course of my trying to protect it, two people have been killed and attempts have been made on the life of another. So I've an added interest. What did you call her?"

"She's a bitch and you'll soon find out," Fraser rasped. "Underneath that sweet and gentle manner of hers she's a devil. Don't make any mistake, she's taking you for a ride." Fraser was pale with rage, his voice quivering with repressed fury. "You can't save her reputation, she hasn't got one. She's a phoney. All she wants is money. She'll use anyone to help her — even you've fallen for it. That woman is a hell-cat. She ruins anyone she touches, anyone who's influenced by her. She'll ruin Mona Lister, she'll ruin *you*."

Anger still rasped in the man's voice but it was a righteous anger. There was no doubt, thought Rollison, that Michael Fraser believed what he was saying.

"All right, I'm duly warned," he said drily. "Now tell me how you know all this, and what proof you have against her."

"There's your proof!" Fraser declared, and he pointed a quivering finger at the brief-case.

"He *didn't* know," the other man said in a strangled voice. "He *was* bluffing. And that's the only real evidence we have. He'll suppress it, destroy it; have you forgotten that he's *defending* the woman?"

Making a tremendous effort, he sprang to his feet and launched himself at Rollison, roaring as he sprang:

"Hit him!"

He was roaring at Jane — and Jane snatched up the telephone to use it as a weapon. Rollison knocked it out of her hand, then, instead of dodging or ducking, met the other broadside on. His left shoulder thudded against his assailant's chest. The man groaned and collapsed across a chair. Rollison spun round to meet an attack from Fraser, but Fraser was still sitting on the floor, looking up at Rollison with a strange expression in his eyes.

"Do something!" screamed Jane.

Fraser ignored her.

The man lying across the chair was groaning.

"Ted, he's hurt you. *Ted!*" She leaned over the stricken man, "Ted, don't. You'll be all right. *Ted!*" There was despair in her voice.

Still watching Fraser, Rollison said: "He's winded, that's all. Straighten him up."

"Rollison," said Fraser, "what would you do if you were convinced that Madam Melinska was a charlatan — no, by God, more than a charlatan — a criminal?"

"Make sure she couldn't fool anybody else," answered Rollison.

"If the charge against her is proved she'll go to prison, won't she?"

"She will indeed."

"What about — what about the girl?"

"That depends on how deeply she's involved."

"She *isn't* involved," Fraser said. "She's an innocent tool in the hands of that infernal woman. Mona's a natural clairvoyante; sometimes she really *can* see into the future, and the Melinska woman uses her to win her victims' confidence before *she* steps in and wrings every penny out of them. If I can convince you of this, will you help Mona? And give up Madam Melinska's defence?"

Rollison nodded.

"Michael, don't trust him," Jane called out.

"I don't see what else we can do," said Fraser. "If Mrs. Abbott's dead then we really are in trouble and we'll need someone to get us out of it. Rollison, Madam Melinska is a confidence trickster on a big scale. She takes nothing for her readings, but by conning her clients into giving her large sums of money which she tells them she'll invest on their behalf, she makes a fortune. She daren't admit she has any money now because this would give the game away — so she's relying on credulous fools — I mean good-hearted people — to put up whatever she needs for her defence. It's all there." He waved a hand towards the brief-case. "Mrs. Abbott has it all down in black and white."

Rollison frowned. "Why did you steal this 'evidence' from Mrs. Abbott? And how did you know Mrs. Abbott had it?"

"I knew because she told me about it. Oh yes, I used to know the Abbotts quite well, and when Mrs. Abbott came to London she looked me up. I lived in Bulawayo for some years, I — I was engaged to the Abbotts' niece, Mona Lister. But then Mona left home and got herself involved with this Melinska woman, and somehow things started going wrong between us. *Another* reason I'd like to get my own back." Fraser added wryly. "Mrs. Abbott was so upset, both about Mona *and* her husband —" He paused. "You know about Abbott's suicide?"

Rollison nodded. "Yes, I heard about it. Carry on."

Fraser frowned. "Where did I get to? Oh yes, Mrs. Abbott was so upset that she decided to collect sufficient evidence to *prove* that Madam Melinska was a fraud. And she has collected it. But I was afraid of what she might say about Mona — when Mona left home and went to live with Madam Melinska Mrs. Abbott turned completely against her, she seemed to hate the girl as much as Madam Melinska — and I was worried in case she implicated her in Madam Melinska's swindles."

"So you persuaded Ted to steal the evidence," Rollison finished for him.

"Yes, I stole it, but I didn't *kill* the woman," insisted the man in the chair. He was looking better now. "I tell you the flat was empty."

Rollison said: "You may have a lot of trouble proving that. Did you see anyone else near the flat?"

"No one I recognised."

"Lucifer Stride, for instance?" Rollison suggested.

He expected the name to cause something of a sensation, but the two men took it without blinking.

"Oh, *Lucy*," Ted said derisively. "*He* wasn't there."

"How well do you know him?" asked Rollison.

"He's my brother — half-brother actually," said Michael Fraser impatiently. "I gave him a job in the office here for a few months, but it didn't work out. *He* certainly wouldn't have anything to do with killing Mrs. Abbott. He might ask for a little — *more* than a little — financial support but — oh, I'm sorry if I sound cold-blooded," Fraser interrupted himself, "but my brother and I don't have much in common. All the same, he wouldn't hurt a fly, and as for *murder* — well, you can certainly rule *him* out. Rollison — *will* you help us expose Madam Melinska?"

"Yes — if she's guilty," said Rollison.

"We can't afford to pay —"

"If Madam Melinska has fooled me I won't deserve any payment," said Rollison. He was aware of a growing uneasiness, a fear that these men might be right about the woman whom his Aunt Gloria trusted so implicitly.

He was interrupted by the ringing of the telephone. Fraser hesitated, glanced at his watch in surprise, then picked up the receiver. A moment later, in even greater surprise, he said: "It's for you, Rollison."

As far as Rollison was aware the only person who knew that he might be here was Olivia Cordman.

11

WELCOME HOME

It was not the Features Editor of *The Day*; it was Jolly. The first syllable of his man's voice warned Rollison that all was not well, and he steeled himself to receive bad news.

"Miss Cordman advised me where you might be, sir. I'm sorry to bother you, but I think you would be well-advised to come home immediately."

"Why?" asked Rollison.

"The – ah – police are in possession," Jolly told him.

"*What?*"

"They are in truth, sir. I tried to communicate with Mr. Grice, but he is said to be out of town."

"What are they doing?" inquired Rollison.

"Searching most extensively, sir. However, I am less concerned with the attitude of the police than with another situation which I think you should see for yourself." Hurriedly, he went on: "Would you care to speak to Chief Inspector Clay, who is in charge here, sir?"

"Just tell him I'll be there as soon as I can," Rollison said.

He rang off on Jolly's "Very good, sir."

He was quite sure that Jolly would have told him more but for Clay's presence. Rollison knew the man slightly – a shrewd and patient detective, but with little imagination and an unyielding faith in the rule book – exactly the type of man whom Grice would second to an investigation into his, Rollison's, activities.

All three members of Space Age Publishing, Limited were watching him; his apprehension must have sounded in his voice. He looked at each in turn, and then said:

"Jane, let me have your own and the men's home addresses and telephone numbers – I may want to get in touch with you. Fraser, I'd like you to send me a written report stating everything you know about Madam Melinska." He turned to the man the others had called Ted. "What's your surname?"

"Jackson."

"I'd like *you* to send me a report of all your movements when you visited Mrs. Abbott, everything you noticed, everyone you saw – a fully detailed description of exactly what happened at the flat."

Jackson looked uneasy. "Do you think the police will get on to me?"

"They might."

"You won't tell them I was —"

"As long as you play ball with me I won't tell the police anything," Rollison said. He took a card from his pocket, with his name—The Honourable Richard Rollison, O.B.E. – and the Gresham Street address on one side, and a pencilled sketch of a top hat, a monocle, a cigarette and a bow tie on the other, and handed it to

Fraser. Once, this had been used as a form of psychological terrorism, a melodramatic threat – *The Toff's on the trail*. There were still times for melodrama, he believed; this might be one of them.

Picking up the brief-case with one hand and taking the slip of paper Jane held out to him with the other, he walked out of the room and across the outer office, leaving the three members of Space Age Publishing, Limited staring after him. Unlocking the passage door, he stepped outside. The automatic self-service lift was still working, and a small door in the large doors of the building had not yet been locked. Rollison stepped out, cautiously.

No one was in the street, but that did not mean that the police weren't at either end, watching; or that the men who had killed Charlie Wray and attempted to kill Lucifer would not be lurking close by. He turned towards the Strand. The brief-case must not be taken to the flat while the police were there, nor must it be taken anywhere the police might search. His club, for instance. Hailing a taxi, he went to Charing Cross station, left the brief-case in a locker, pocketed the key and looked about cautiously, but no one appeared to be paying him any particular attention.

Outside, he bought a newspaper.

His own face, Madam Melinska's and Mona's stared up at him; and there were front page headlines.

TOFF TO THE RESCUE

£100 BAIL FOR MADAM MELINSKA

GALLANTRY IN COURT

The story, as a story, was factual enough; what Rollison hadn't expected was the space and prominence the evening papers gave to it.

There was a long queue for taxis, so he walked down Villiers Street, and through the Embankment Gardens to his car. A ticket was wedged under his windscreen-wiper and he realised that he had only put two six-pences into the parking meter. He drove off very thoughtfully, half wishing he had looked in the brief-case.

Half an hour later he turned off Piccadilly and was in sight of Gresham Terrace. The first thing to startle him was the sight of the policemen, three of them; the second, the stream of people; the third, the fact that the police were sending cars straight past the end of Gresham Terrace. His heart thumped. Had there been an acci-dent, or —

A policeman came up to him.

"The street's barred for the next hour or so, sir. You can only get into Gresham Terrace on foot. I —" the man broke off. "Aren't *you* Mr. Rollison?"

"Yes. I'll get rid of the car and come back."

"One of our men will look after the car for you, sir. Chief Inspector Clay would like to see you as soon as possible. He's waiting at your place."

Rollison looked along Gresham Terrace.

It was a seething mass of people, mostly women. At this end of the street they were fairly thinly spread but farther along they were packed so solidly that no one could pass. Two or three cars were completely hemmed in; until the crowd was cleared there would be no chance for them to move.

"That's a welcome *if* you like," the policeman said

with reluctant admiration. "They're waiting for *you*, sir. Lot of half-wits!"

Rollison chuckled and then said: "I don't want to run that gauntlet, I'd better go the back way." He opened the far door of the car and stepped out, but as he did so a middle-aged woman coming along the street cried:

"There he is!"

Someone else shouted: "There's the Toff!"

"The Toff!"

"You haven't a hope," said the policeman, *sotto voce*.

Rollison stood by the side of the car and watched the crowd bear down on him. Suddenly he was surrounded, engulfed, enmeshed in hundreds of seemingly bodiless hands stretched frantically to clutch his own.

Rollison thought with alarm: "They'll mob me."

Then he thought: "They're here to help."

"*You will get help from many unexpected sources.*"

"Sir!" hissed the policeman, "Chief Inspector —"

"God bless you, sir."

"*She* didn't cheat anyone! She couldn't do it."

"She's an angel, that woman is."

"Don't let them put her in prison, Mr. Rollison."

"*Sir*, Chief Inspector Clay wants —" The policeman tried again.

Rollison stood perfectly still by the side of the car, with the crowd pressing nearer and harder; it would need only a sudden surge from behind to crush him and those nearest to him against the Bentley, and once that happened disaster could follow.

Very clearly, Rollison cried: "What I would like to do

is to talk to you all from my window — if I could just get through to my flat . . ."

"The Toff wants to get through."

". . . a speech."

"Make room."

"Clear a path."

"The Toff's going to talk to us!"

"Stand aside, there," the policeman said, as if he did not believe he would have the slightest effect.

"Stand back!" a little woman shouted shrilly.

Another began to push.

"Make a path."

"A path!"

"Get back!"

"Link arms — make a chain . . . chain . . . chain . . ."

And as if by magic a path appeared among the crowd, as those standing nearest to Rollison linked arms in time-honoured policeman fashion and pressed back on those behind. There were outbursts of cheering, and two men started to sing "For he's a jolly good fellow." Immediately the refrain was taken up by the crowd, louder and louder, until the whole street was singing.

At the window of the big living-room at Rollison's flat, Chief Inspector Clay stared down, watching the seething, excited people, seeing the way they moved aside for Rollison, noting the respect, the affection, almost the love they had for him. After a few minutes he turned round and bumped against Jolly, who had also been staring down, his eyes quite moist.

"Nothing like this can ever have happened before," muttered Clay. "It's crazy."

"It's happened at least three times to my knowledge, sir," Jolly said. "I remember —" He broke off, for Clay was at the telephone, and turned back to watch the scene below. Rollison was now almost directly beneath the window. The singing rose to a crescendo as he reached the steps leading up to the front door downstairs.

Jolly moved to open the door of the flat. Two of Clay's men were in the hall, looking ill-at-ease. Jolly opened the door and went to the head of the stairs. The noise was fainter here, and sounds from the downstair hall were sharp and clear; a key in the lock, footsteps, the closing of the door, then Rollison's footsteps on the stairs.

Then a man said clearly:

"Stay there, Rollison."

Rollison, out of sight, seemed to catch his breath.

Jolly, startled and alarmed, stepped forward. "Who are you?" he heard Rollison ask.

"Never mind who I am. What did you find at Mrs. Abbott's flat?"

Jolly began to creep very slowly down the stairs.

"Mrs. Abbott — dead."

"If you try to be funny *you'll* soon be dead."

"Put that gun away and stop talking like a fool." Jolly, nearer now, detected a steely note in Rollison's voice.

"Don't call *me* a fool. All those screaming half-wits out there — *they're* the fools. And they're wrong, that damned fortune-teller has fooled them. However, that's their funeral — but it will be yours too if you don't tell me what you found at Mrs. Abbott's."

Jolly held his breath as he peered down the well of the staircase.

He saw his master and a tall, dark-haired young man; and he saw the gun in the young man's hand. If he touched the trigger, there wouldn't be a chance for Rollison.

Quite calmly, Jolly called:

"Excuse me, sir."

On the instant the young man looked up, and Rollison drove his fist into the unprotected stomach. As the gun clattered to the floor, Rollison stopped the other from falling, and glanced up with a smile which Jolly would treasure for a very long time.

"Are you all right, sir?"

"Yes. Come and look after this chap, will you? Give me ten minutes or so, and then bring him up to the flat."

"Certainly, sir." Jolly hurried down the stairs and picked up the gun, and Rollison turned to his assailant. "Go upstairs with Jolly, and let the police think you've just come to see me. Don't try any tricks or I'll throw the book at you." Bounding past Jolly and the stranger, he ran up the remaining stairs towards his flat.

Clay and two other men were standing in the hall, and Rollison beamed at them as if he hadn't a trouble in the world.

"Won't keep you long," he said, and strode through to the living-room. In a moment he was leaning out of the window. As his head appeared there was another roar of cheering.

At last the crowd fell silent.

At last Rollison was able to make himself heard.

"I promise you that justice *will* be done to Madam Melinska and to Mona Lister. I promise you —"

It was as if everyone in the street went mad, the waving, the cheering, were so furious. Even when he had spoken to them five times, another roar for him came as fast as he could shut the window; but gradually the crowd grew silent, and the police filtered in and took complete control.

"Now what can I do to help you?" Rollison asked Chief Inspector Clay.

12

FRIEND INTO FOE

Rollison looked blankly into Clay's eyes, silently echoing "arrest". Clay was hostile and in a way defiant. Slowly, Rollison began to relax; suddenly, he realised how lucky it was that he had left the stolen papers in the station locker; that was a break in a thousand. He saw the puzzlement in the Yard man's eyes as he grinned.

"Well, well," he said. "It's quite a time since the Yard made that mistake. All right, officer, I'll come quietly – but I'd like a couple of hours' grace."

"You'll come with me, *now*."

Rollison's eyes were still laughing.

"Why not ask Grice for my grace?"

"Mr. Grice is not concerned in this case."

"He will be," Rollison said. "Believe me, he will be. You know, this is the most remarkable tribute to Madam Melinska. She said my friends would become my foes, or words to that effect, but that I would get help from unexpected sources. I wonder where it will come from next. Chief Inspector —"

"I'm not here to talk," Clay growled.

"No," Rollison said. "Nor to slow down your rate of promotion."

"If you're threatening me —" Clay's eyes flashed.

"Don't be a fool, man," Rollison said lightly. "Of course I'm not threatening you. But if you arrest me and the Court dismisses the case in the morning, won't it count against you?" When Clay didn't answer, Rollison went on: "You know damn well it would take years to live down. Yes, I realise you wouldn't have got a warrant unless you thought it was justified, but events *can* make a clever man look foolish. What's the charge?"

"Illegal entry."

"*What?*"

"I needn't keep saying it — the charge is illegal entry."

"At Mrs. Abbott's?"

"Where else have you forced entry?" demanded Clay, sharply.

Rollison thought: "He certainly isn't a fool." He said: "So you'll hold me on that for twenty-four hours and hope you can prove I murdered Mrs. Abbott. Tell me, do you *really* believe I murdered her?"

Clay drew a deep breath.

"Mr. Richard Rollison, it is my duty to —"

Rollison rasped: "Do you think I murdered Mrs. Abbott?"

"That's nothing to do with the matter in hand."

Rollison thought: "I can't shift him, he's as stubborn as a mule." They were staring at each other, hostility mutual now, until Rollison said abruptly: "May I make one telephone call?"

"Provided I know who you're calling."

"My solicitor," Rollison said shortly.

"Well —"

Clay was interrupted by a commotion at the front door, as Jolly came inside, ushering the stranger who had threatened Rollison on the stairs. Two detectives turned to Clay, not knowing what to do, as Jolly said in vexed tones:

"I'm sorry, sir, but this is Jones, who applied for the post as valet. Shall *I* interview him, sir?"

Rollison nodded. "Yes, will you do that, Jolly? I may be out for a while."

"Very well, sir. This way, Jones —" Jolly led the way to his quarters, the stranger followed bemusedly, and Clay appeared to be completely unsuspicious.

Rollison picked up the telephone and dialled a Temple Bar number. He could think of only one man who might be able to help him in this situation, a member of a firm of London solicitors with a big practice in criminal law. There was always the risk that the man he wanted would be out, but he concealed his uncertainty when a girl answered.

"Kemp, Davidson, Kemp and Davis."

"Mr. Roger Kemp, please – this is Richard Rollison."

"Who – *who*, sir?" The girl's voice rose. "Mr. Rollison, the – the *Toff*?"

"That's what they call me."

"I'll put you through, Mr. Rollison, but I would like to say how wonderful it was of you to help Madam Melinska this morning. She is a remarkable woman, and no more guilty than I am, if you'll forgive me saying so,

sir . . . Here's Mr. Roger . . . Oh, Mr. Roger, it's the
To—it's Mr. *Rollison*."

A man with a very deep voice said:

"That's the first time in ten years I've ever known
Betty say a word out of place, Rolly. What influence did
you exert?"

"Astrological," Rollison answered.

"What—oh!" Kemp chuckled. "She's a star-gazer
too, is she? I didn't know until this morning how many
women *were* fooled by that nonsense. Want some help
with the Madam Melinska case? You obviously need
it."

"Roger," Rollison said, "I'm likely to be at Cannon
Row in an hour or less on a charge of illegal entry. I
want a hearing tonight—within the hour if possible.
I've a lot to do and I can't do it with this charge hanging
over my head . . . Did I force entry? My dear fellow—
you know damn well I didn't . . . Well, there was a
strong smell of burning and *someone* had to get into that
place pretty quickly . . . My dear chap, the magistrate
will dismiss the charge in sixty seconds flat —" Rollison
did not so much as glance at Clay, but he was aware of
the detective's fixed, tense stare. "All I need is a quick
hearing . . . You will? Good man! If I'm not at Cannon
Row, presumably I'll be at the Yard . . . Well, until
I'm actually charged I suppose it's no use getting the
magistrate . . . hold on a minute, have a word with
Chief Inspector Clay."

He handed the telephone to Clay, who took it with
obvious reluctance and hesitated. Then he covered the
mouthpiece with the palm of his hand.

"Will you undertake to stay here while I refer to my superiors, Mr. Rollison?"

"Provided I'm free to go out in a couple of hours," Rollison agreed. Inwardly he exulted, outwardly he showed no sign at all of triumph. "Nothing I need more than a couple of hours rest, and I can see that chap Jones. I —"

Clay was saying to Kemp: "No, sir, there was a misunderstanding, I have not yet made the arrest, I'm going to refer to my superiors, sir . . . Yes, I fully understand." He put down the receiver and looked at Rollison with some resentment. "I shall leave men outside, back and front," he said warningly.

Rollison said quietly: "My word on it, I won't leave here until I've heard from you. Will you do something for me at the Yard?"

"*For* you?" Clay was taken aback.

"I need to know all I can about Mrs. Abbott, her late husband, their family, business and background. Now she's been murdered you'll have to check these points, and I think they might help me to clear Madam Melinska. Normally, Mr. Grice would let me know anything which had no direct bearing on the case. Will you do so?"

Clay still looked startled. "I need to get permission."

"I'll be grateful if you will," Rollison said.

Clay nodded, and turned away. Two minutes later he and his men had left the flat, Jolly appearing as if by magic as soon as the front door had closed on them.

"Is the man quite mad?" he demanded.

"Just over-zealous and convinced I've been treated too leniently for too long," Rollison said. "They'll hold off unless they get something much more specific. What's your man got to say for himself?"

Jolly answered: "Not a word, sir."

"Let me have a good look at him," Rollison said, and added: "That valet idea was very clever."

"Thank you, sir," said Jolly, almost smugly. "It seemed one way to prevent the police from suspecting that we were keeping him prisoner. I'll go and get him, sir – I locked him in the spare-room bathroom."

The spare-room bathroom had a ventilator but no window.

Rollison moved to the living-room window and looked down, seeing Clay striding to his car, glancing neither to right nor left. The crowds were beginning to disperse but there was still a large number of people in the street, and it passed through Rollison's mind that they could quite easily have mobbed Clay had they known about the warrant.

Suddenly he heard Jolly call:

"Will you come here, sir?"

There was a note of alarm in his voice, and Rollison moved swiftly. Jolly appeared at the spare-room door.

"He's unconscious, sir."

"What?"

"It's almost as if he – was asphyxiated, sir."

Rollison said: "He can't have been." He thrust his way across the bedroom and into the bathroom, sniffing: the air was clear, there was no lack of oxygen. The stranger was sitting on the floor, head lolling on his chest, arms draped by his side. Rollison felt his pulse; it was steady enough, but faint. He hoisted him up and carried him into the spare room, laying him on the bed. Jolly had already loosened his collar and tie, and now Rollison gently pushed up one of his eyelids.

Jolly moved forward to peer at the pupil. "A *pin-point*, sir!"

"Morphia," Rollison said with relief. "He came prepared, didn't he? Rather than answer questions he put himself to sleep. But he'll wake up, Jolly. Go through his clothes, find out what he has in his pockets, and let me know. I've got some telephoning to do."

"Madam Melinska is perfectly all right, Richard," said Lady Hurst. "And has every confidence in you. I hope it isn't misplaced."

"So do I," said Rollison earnestly. "Has Mona said anything?"

"I am afraid she is rather a sullen child. So many pretty ones are."

"Win her round," urged Rollison. "Turn on your charm, Aunt Gloria, I've never needed it more. Find out all you can about her aunt and uncle, friends, family and relations. And please, *soon*," he pleaded.

"I will certainly try, if you think it will be of any use."

"It will — and *I've* every confidence in *you*," Rollison said, warmly. "*Now*, Aunt —"

He was smiling when he rang off.

Jolly appeared as he replaced the receiver.

"He has removed every identifying mark from his clothes, sir, and there is none in his pockets – no clue at all to his identity, unless this is a clue, sir."

Jolly held out his hand, palm uppermost. On it was a small coin, so small that Rollison nearly dropped it when he picked it up. Then he said in surprise:

"It's one of our old threepenny bits – no, not ours, South African – a ticky, didn't they call them? South African, Jolly."

"And South Africa has a common border with Rhodesia, sir," Jolly observed.

"Yes indeed. Put it back where you found it – he needn't know we know about it. And now, how about a quick cup of coffee – I may be too busy for dinner."

It was nearly an hour later that Chief Inspector Clay telephoned.

"In view of new information which has become available, Mr. Rollison, we are not proceeding with the charge," he announced.

"Thanks," said Rollison, "very understanding of you."

"On the other matter, inquiries are in hand and any information which is not confidential will be passed on."

"Thanks again," Rollison said more warmly. "Is anything known?"

"Harold Abbott committed suicide, sir."

"Any close relatives?"

"The Abbotts were a childless couple," said Clay. "As far as we can ascertain the only surviving relative seems to be a niece, Miss Mona Lister."

"What did Abbott do for a living?"

"He appears to have been of independent means," answered Clay. "If I have further information I will telephone you in the morning."

"You're very good," Rollison said gratefully.

He rang off, went into the spare room to examine the stranger, whose condition was unchanged, and called Jolly. "If this fellow doesn't come round in an hour, send for Dr. Webber. I think he's all right, but we'd better make sure. I don't know when I'll be back."

"Mr. Rollison, sir —"

"Yes, I *will* be careful. Especially as I'm going to use your car."

"This is a very peculiar case, sir."

"It is indeed."

"You can trust no one at all."

"No one at all," echoed Rollison. "You may be right. If you really get worried, call Miss Cordman's flat. If things work out as I think they will, I shall almost certainly trust her."

"Not too far, sir, *please*," Jolly begged.

Rollison went out by the back door and the fire escape, to evade those people still gathered in Gresham Terrace. Jolly's Morris, black, shiny and immaculate, was housed in a nearby garage; one of the policemen had put the Bentley in alongside it. Slipping quickly into the driving seat, Rollison swung the Morris in the direction of Charing Cross. Pulling up outside the station, he strode inside and took the brief-case out of the locker. He then went back to the car, drove to the

STARS FOR THE TOFF

Embankment, pulled up once again, and at long last opened the case.

Inside, was a thick file of papers.

On the outside, it was marked: *Madam Melinska. Dossier and Proof.*

13

"DOSSIER AND PROOF"

Rollison read until the light began to fade and he could read no more. Twelve men and women were listed in the dossier; each had been a client of Madame Melinska, each had been persuaded to give her a substantial sum for investment on their behalf. In every instance this money had disappeared.

No cases had been brought, some of the victims not wishing it to be known they had consulted a fortune-teller, others not wishing it to be known that they had lost money, or been made fools of.

Rollison sat back and reflected. It was chilly; once or twice he shivered.

After a few moments he left the car, carrying the brief-case with him, and walked to a telephone kiosk on the other side of the Embankment. The white hulls of the old sailing ships which had carried countless heroes on countless adventures, gleamed in the dusk. Opposite, silent, ghost-like, was the Temple. Across the river the Festival Hall was bright with welcome lights, and the new Shell House was like a diamond corsage draped on the sky.

He dialled Olivia Cordman's number. Brrr-brrr; brrr-brrr: the ringing went on and on for what seemed a very long time. A shadowy figure approached, looking sinister, misshapen, in the half-light; a man waited close by, jingling coins. Brrr-brrr; brrr-brrr; brrr-brrr – Better give up, thought Rollison. Pity.

"Who the devil's *that*?" demanded Olivia in obvious exasperation. "I can't even take a bath without —"

" – a hungry man asking to be fed."

There was a pause. Then: "Who *is* that?"

"My aunt calls me Richard."

"Who – oh, *Rolly*." Pleasure took the place of exasperation. "Are you serious? *Are* you hungry?"

"Famished. I thought – " added Rollison diffidently – "that you *might* like to cook me supper."

"I'd love to, but it will have to be bacon and eggs. That's all I've got."

"Just the supper we can talk over," said Rollison approvingly.

Olivia laughed. "Was there ever a time when you didn't want information? But honestly, I'll love to see you. When will you be here?"

"Is twenty minutes all right?"

"Make it half an hour," pleaded Olivia.

"Half an hour it will be."

"That's lovely!" She rang off, giving Rollison the impression of simple delight; and he remembered Jolly's warning. Smiling, he went out of the kiosk and into the road – and a car, parked without lights, started up with a venomous roar. Suddenly the headlights were switched full on, blinding him. For a split second he could not decide whether to leap forward or back, the glare was mesmerising, terror pounded in his heart. Then he flung himself forward. The brief-case went flying, the roar of the engine was deafening, and Rollison felt a sensation almost of numbness as he fell full length on the hard concrete. As he fell, the powerful lights and a dark shape passed barely an inch behind him, and the roaring died away.

Another car drew up, brakes squealing, and two men leaped out of it. Rollison grunted and groaned as he staggered to his feet. The two men helped to steady him.

"Are you all right?"

"My God, that was a miracle!"

"The crazy fool!"

"Must be drunk."

"How many were in it?" Rollison asked.

"Just the driver."

"*Must* be drunk."

"*Are* you all right?" the first man repeated.

"Er—yes. Bloodied but in one piece," Rollison said. "Have you seen my brief-ca—ah!" A woman held it out to him. "Thank you very much. I—ah—must look where I'm going. Sorry to cause such a sensation."

"If you're all right —"

"It wasn't *your* fault."

"Have you a car?"

"Are you all right to drive?"

"Are you sure? I'll gladly take you —"

"Or you could get a taxi."

As they talked, still excited and greatly incensed,

they moved along the road until they reached the Morris. Bending his back to get inside was excruciatingly painful, and once in, Rollison sat back, sweating. The barrage of questions started again. They were embarrassingly helpful.

Help from many unexpected sources.

"I'm sure I can manage," Rollison said.

"You ought to report it, you know."

"Oh, no harm's done."

"He must have been mad."

Or a murderer, thought Rollison.

"Well if you're quite sure . . ."

They stood and watched as he drove off, handling the controls stiffly at first but gradually improving. He went cautiously to Cheyne Walk, where every parking space seemed full, then found a spot outside Olivia Cordman's front door. Normally he would have slipped in without trouble. Now, turning to look round was like knifing himself in the ribs; it was even worse getting out. He looked about and saw an old-fashioned lamp-post with a bar just beneath the lamp, and eyed it speculatively; swinging was supposed to be good for a strained back. He stretched up gingerly, managed to get a hold, and hoisted himself high.

Soon he was swinging with greater pain at his shoulders than at his back, and when he walked again he was more sore than in pain. He glanced at his watch; it was exactly half an hour since he had telephoned Olivia.

She was on the seventh floor; happily there was a lift.

"Why, come in!" she said. Then she caught her breath. "Your jacket's torn!" she exclaimed.

"You mean there's some left?"

"And you're bleeding!"

"Just a scratch."

"Well anyway, you ought to have it seen to." She took his arm firmly and led him along a passage and into the bathroom, sat him down, and studied him in the bright light. Then she poured water, and ministered, talking about nothing in particular, until at last she ushered him into the sitting-room.

"Will you eat first and talk after, or talk first and eat after?"

"Could I drink first?" asked Rollison, sinking into an easy chair.

"Oh, what an ass I am. What'll you have?"

Rollison settled for a whisky, and soon began to talk. Olivia sat on a pouffe in front of him, peering earnestly up into his eyes. She looked appalled when he described the accident, but when he told her of the Good Samaritans her face lit up.

"So it *did* come true — Madam Melinska's help from unexpected sources! You *can't* doubt her after this."

"Can't I?" said Rollison grimly.

Olivia stared at him for several seconds, her expression slowly changing. The gay, almost child-like delight faded, she seemed to grow older, more severe, more authoritative. Her eyes narrowed to give an impression of great severity, and when she began to speak it was as if she were about to make an announcement of supreme importance.

"*You* are a Virgo," she announced.

Rollison said, bewildered: "A what?"

"A Virgo. When were you born?"

"August the twenty-third, but —"

"I knew it," said Olivia, as if pronouncing a death sentence. "You were born on the cusp, too. Leo gives you your arrogance and Virgo your scepticism. *Only* a Virgo would doubt Madam Melinska after *this*. Your East End friends desert you, and immediately you get a seething mob of helpers outside your flat. The police turn against you, and perfect strangers come to your rescue. This is *exactly* what Madam Melinska prophesied."

Rollison said mildly: "I see what you mean. How quickly can you read?"

"Very quickly. It's my profession."

"If I cook the bacon and eggs will you read this?" Rollison asked. After a short but explicit account of how he had obtained it, he took the file out of the brief-case and handed it to Olivia, stood up, and made his way to the kitchen — small, modern, spick-and-span. In one frying-pan was bacon, in another, four uncracked eggs. On a table were fat, salt and pepper. Rollison lit two gas-rings, and began to cook as Jolly had taught him years ago. He could move freely now, and went about the task with slow deliberation, going through the whole case in his mind. Once or twice he peeped into the sitting-room.

Olivia Cordman was sitting upright in an armchair, poring over the file. Her spectacles had peach-coloured frames, and gave her a slightly school-mistressy appearance. Her only movement was the occasional wrinkling of her forehead, causing a straight furrow between her eyes.

Rollison took two small trays from a shelf, and soon he was laying a plate of steaming eggs and bacon on each. He checked that he had everything, then carried the trays proudly into the sitting-room. Olivia did not look up. He placed her tray on a small table by her side, his own on the pouffe in front of his easy chair. She did not appear to notice.

He began to eat. "Hm, very good."

"It's dreadful."

"Don't let it get cold."

"It's shameful."

"It certainly will be, if you let that bacon congeal."

She looked up, glaring.

"This *isn't* funny."

"It won't be, if you —"

She scowled at him, then, suddenly, her face cleared, she put the papers down, gave a little coo of satisfaction, and said:

"You've cooked supper—oh, you shouldn't have. Why, it's terrible, inviting someone to supper and then letting them cook it. But it looks beautiful." She sprayed pepper liberally over her eggs and bacon, and began to eat with gusto. "Who taught you to cook? — You ought to do it more often. I'll bet it was Jolly, he's out of this world—an anachronism, poor dear. A bit like *you*," she added, her smile robbing the words of any sting. "You're both links with the past, and sometimes I *hate* the present." She ate for a minute or two, and then said with troubled earnestness: "*Can* these beastly reports be true?"

"They certainly can be."

"Then — *are* they?"

"If I'd seen them before, I don't think I would have been so quick to bail the ladies out," Rollison said.

"*Twelve* people advised to invest in Space Age Publishing and then cheated out of their savings — I just can't believe it. And that poor Mr. Abbott —" Olivia stopped.

"Not a pretty record," said Rollison grimly.

"And when he died, Mrs. Abbott employed private detectives to dig out everything they could about Madam Melinska?"

"Yes."

"And this is what they found? I *can't* believe it."

Rollison frowned. "Well, either it's true, or Madam Melinska *is* being framed — like the girl said. But if it is true and this story became public property, it wouldn't do Madam Melinska any good at all. I believe someone broke into Mrs. Abbott's flat to steal this dossier — which had, of course, already been stolen by our friend Ted Jackson — if Jackson's telling the truth, that is. Interrupted by Mrs. Abbott, the thief lost his head, panicked, and strangled her — then set the place on fire to try to cover his tracks. Either that or he intended to both steal the dossier *and* silence Mrs. Abbott."

Olivia shivered. "Oh it's dreadful, dreadful. And what's even worse —" She paused, and Rollison waited with awed fascination to hear what was worse than murder — "what's even worse, is the possibility that

Madam Melinska might prove to be a fake. It's terrible
—no one would believe in fortune-telling again for
years. Every fortune-teller would be absolutely dis-
credited. It's bad enough when half the people you
meet are sceptics, and at best tolerate what they consider to be *your* folly, but if Madam Melinska *is* guilty—"

She broke off, and in that moment Rollison knew
exactly how much this mattered to her. She was not
exaggerating; she meant exactly what she said; and
then she caught her breath and cried out:

"Oh, *no!*"

"Now what?" asked Rollison.

"She *knew* about the attack on you—she warned you,
didn't she, she told you there would be danger. Oh, my
goodness, this gets worse. If she *is* guilty, then *she* must
have plotted your death. You know, Rolly, there's only
one thing to do. You've *got* to prove that she's innocent."

"Whether she is or not?"

"You know what I mean. Rolly, we must go and see
her at once. *I'll* know whether she's lying. And I dare
say you will, too," Olivia added kindly.

"Ah," said Rollison. "But will the police?" After a
pause, he added: "Give me a pencil and some paper, will
you, and I'll take some notes. It'll be safer to leave the
actual reports here . . ."

14

"TO TELL THE TRUTH"

Madam Melinska sat in an armchair, hands folded on her lap, face set in repose. As he talked, Rollison studied every feature and every line, and in spite of all he had read in the dossier he had a feeling of utter absurdity; it was ludicrous to suspect this woman of the crimes about which he was now talking. He went through them one after another, giving a précis of each. His aunt sat upright in a high-backed chair, her face set in disapproval. Mona Lister lay back on a couch. Olivia sat on a stool, one hand at her chin, her brow furrowed.

"And according to this dossier," said Rollison uncomfortably, rustling his notes to show his listeners that he was perfectly at ease, "you first advised your clients to make substantial investments in certain companies, *then* you persuaded them to hand you the amounts involved so that you might make the investments on their behalf. These investments were never made."

"I was certainly consulted by all twelve persons you mention," agreed Madam Melinska. "But in such consultations I am only the medium through which advice is given. I am completely unaware of what is said through me, Mr. Rollison."

"So you did give these twelve people consultations?"

"Yes. As I would you or anyone else troubled about the future and whom I might perhaps be able to help."

"I see. And each of these twelve people gave you large sums of money which they understood you would invest for them?"

"That is not true, Mr. Rollison."

"Then they lied?"

"So it would seem."

"Madam Melinska, I can believe that *one* of those people might lie — even though there seems little reason for his doing so — but that all *twelve* should lie is very hard to believe."

She smiled. "I agree, Mr. Rollison. It *is* very hard to believe. So hard to believe that I do not in fact believe it."

Rollison frowned. "This isn't funny!"

"No," agreed Madam Melinska, gently. "It *is*, however, strange that you who are defending me should accuse me."

"On the strength of these reports," said Rollison, "you will undoubtedly be committed for trial and may well be found guilty."

"That would be a grave miscarriage of justice."

"But it will happen unless you can prove they're untrue."

"Or unless *you* can prove it," she returned, mildly. "Mr. Rollison, you are not distressing me. I am quite resigned to whatever should happen, what is to be is written in the stars. But I am afraid you *are* distressing our friends."

Rollison was jolted into awareness of the presence of the others; he had forgotten them, so deeply absorbed was he in this woman's manner. Was she a consummate liar, or was she absolutely convinced of her powers as a seer? He saw his aunt's frown of concentration and felt sure she was asking herself the same question. Olivia jumped up.

"Rolly, you can't deny that Madam Melinska prophesied that you would be in grave danger, and you *have* been; and that you'd be deserted by your friends, and you *have* been, both by the East Enders *and* the police."

"It doesn't take supernatural powers to know there's danger in this affair, and that if I help a star-gazer I'll put the backs up of some people and win the support of others. All that could be intelligent guesswork. Look," Rollison turned from Olivia to Madam Melinska. "This dossier exists. Even without it, you would be in trouble. With it, you are in very deep trouble indeed. Consequently you have a very strong motive for having it stolen from Mrs. Abbott. As she no doubt knew what was in it, you also had a good motive for wanting her dead. And for wanting me dead, should you have discovered that it was in my possession. And someone certainly tried to kill me a while back."

"But no one stole it from you!" cried Olivia, her eyes suddenly radiant. "So it couldn't have been because of the dossier they tried to kill you."

"A lot of people were about."

"Richard," pronounced Lady Hurst, "are you being absolutely fair to Madam Melinska?"

"Aunt," said Rollison grimly, "before you and I commit ourselves further, we have to be absolutely certain that she isn't fooling us. I —"

"No!" cried Mona Lister, loudly and clearly, making everyone turn towards her. She lay back on the couch as if asleep. "No, Lucy, don't go in there — *don't*." Her voice rose in obvious fear. "Don't go in, he's waiting for you — behind the door. *Don't!*"

Rollison thought: "Lucy? *Lucifer Stride?*"

"*Don't go in!*"

Madam Melinska sprang up from her chair, reached the girl and put a hand on her forehead. Mona began to twist and turn — but her eyes were still closed. Madam Melinska knelt down beside the couch.

"*Come back to me,*" she said quietly. "*Come back to me.*"

The girl fell silent and the writhing ceased. She opened her eyes. The older woman began to stroke her forehead very gently and after a few seconds she asked:

"Where was this happening, Mona?"

"I — I don't know. But I saw Lucy —"

"Do you mean Lucifer Stride?"

"Yes. I saw him go up some stairs and ring the door bell. Another man was on the other side of the door, and someone else was coming up the stairs, carrying a weapon. It was — awful." The girl's voice was faint now, and she looked very pale.

"Did you see anyone else, child?"

"No. No, I didn't. I only saw —" Mona frowned as

if with a great effort at recollection. "A top hat — yes, a top hat — on a wall, high up on a wall."

"My God!" gasped Rollison. "That's my Trophy Wall!" He swung round towards the door. As he reached the landing Olivia came out after him, then ran ahead. By the time he reached the square, she was at the wheel of Jolly's Morris, lights on, the engine running. He slipped in beside her; almost before he closed the door Olivia was moving off. There was no traffic, and every light was green for them; in less than ten minutes they turned into Gresham Terrace.

As they did so, a car engine roared, not far away. Rollison had a spasm of fear, for it was the same noise he had heard as the car had tried to run him down. Lights blazed at the far corner of the street.

"There they are!" Rollison cried. "By Jove, I think it's the car that tried to run down Lucifer!"

"We'll catch them!" Olivia rammed her foot down on the accelerator, and the Morris raced forward.

"Hold it!" cried Rollison. "Jolly may be —"

Before he could add "hurt" Olivia's foot was on the brake and he was thrust forward. As he straightened up Olivia stretched across to his door and it swung open.

"You see to Jolly, I'll go after this little lot," she said, and began to push Rollison out. She was so tiny yet so fierce that even as he staggered on to the pavement he was half-laughing at her; but it *was* only half-laughing. Fear for Jolly drove him into the silent house, up the deserted staircase, to the top flat, where light streamed from the open door. There was no sound. His heart in his mouth, Rollison went in; the hall was quite normal — except that in the doorway leading to the living-room, there was a foot.

The shoe was long, narrow, pointed, brown: not Jolly's.

Rollison gritted his teeth as he went forward and Lucifer Stride's body gradually came in sight. He was stretched out at full length, his head on one side, a heavy bruise on the temple. Rollison knelt down and felt his pulse; it was beating, although faintly. Afraid of what he would see next, Rollison looked quickly into each room; there was no sign of Jolly until he approached the spare bedroom.

The door was wide open.

Jolly was kneeling by the side of the bed, his head bent forward over the counterpane, one arm bent under him, the other dangling by his side. There was no sign of the prisoner. Rollison went to him, still fearfully, and took his wrist. Thank God *he* was alive, too, and his pulse seemed steady. He raised him, gently, and as his head lolled backwards, saw the red bruises on his throat; someone had seized Jolly from behind and almost choked the life out of him. Rollison laid him on the bed, undid his collar and waistband and took off his shoes. Then he piled blankets on him, made sure he could breathe freely, and went back to the living-room.

Lucifer Stride stirred.

Rollison moved to the telephone, lifted it, and dialled 230 1212. When a girl said: "Scotland Yard," he asked:

"Is Chief Inspector Clay in, do you know?"

"Yes, sir. He just made a call. Who wants him?"

"Richard Rollison."

"Mr. Rollison!" The tone suggested that there were followers of Madam Melinska and the stars even at the Yard. "One moment, sir."

In that moment, Clay said with heavy but welcome humour, "Good evening, Mr. Rollison. Decided to give yourself up?"

"Decided to hide nothing from you," Rollison said drily. "While I was out . . ."

Almost before Rollison had finished Clay said: "I'll arrange for an ambulance and a doctor, and I'll come over myself."

He was on the spot in twelve minutes, and an ambulance arrived almost immediately afterwards, with a long-limbed young doctor, brisk and competent. He examined Lucifer Stride's head wound carefully.

"Could be a case for brain surgery, that was some blow." He stood up and went to the telephone, signalling to the ambulance men to put Stride on to the stretcher. Rollison watched and listened, as Clay and his men searched for clues and the doctor made what arrangements were needed with the hospital. He was thinking, now, more of Olivia Cordman than of Lucifer Stride; was impatient for the telephone to be free, so that if Olivia called she could get through.

The doctor put down the receiver. "Well, that's all settled. And now, what about the other fellow? No, no, don't show me, I'll find him." He disappeared in the direction of the spare bedroom. A few minutes later he was back. "He'll be okay. It's the first chap I'm worried about." He followed the stretcher downstairs.

Rollison felt a surge of relief. Thank God Jolly was all right, he thought, he could have been badly hurt — these men were undoubtedly killers.

Killers . . . And Olivia had gone chasing after them . . .

Rollison glanced anxiously at the telephone, but it remained silent.

Clay crossed to him.

"What made you suspicious, Mr. Rollison?"

Rollison answered in a tone of mingled wonder and anger. "A nineteen-year-old girl 'saw' this happening from a mile away, and I took her seriously."

"You mean — Miss Lister?" Clay looked astounded. "Good God!"

"Precisely."

"She actually *saw* — oh, it must be some kind of trick."

"Oh, no," Rollison said. "Not this one. Whether we like it or not, she went into some sort of trance — I thought she was asleep, actually — and then began to shout in distress. Even if she'd *known* what was going to happen, she couldn't have known the precise *time* it would happen, and — but she didn't know." He looked at Clay, his eyes troubled. "She *couldn't* have known."

Clay said stubbornly: "All right then, it was a kind of premonition "

Rollison pointed to the Trophy Wall.

"In that premonition she saw that top hat — and she saw Lucifer Stride being attacked." He forced a laugh.

"Oh, it doesn't matter. Jolly was attacked, and she didn't see that." There was no reason to say anything about the stranger he had left locked in the spare bedroom. If Clay had any idea of this he would certainly be very awkward indeed, and the knowledge that he had had a prisoner and lost him was cause enough for chagrin. If only Ebbutt's men had been prepared to help, the flat would have been watched and this could never have happened.

And Olivia Cordman wouldn't be missing.

Was 'missing' too strong a word? Or was the situation serious enough to make it necessary for him to tell Clay to look for the Features Editor of *The Day* if she didn't ring through soon.

The telephone bell rang, and he snatched up the receiver.

"Rollison." But it wasn't Olivia.

"Richard," said Lady Hurst, "I trust there was no cause for alarm."

"Oh —" Rollison tried to cloak his disappointment — "Jolly's all right."

"And the young man?"

"He's on his way to hospital, and we should know his condition in a couple of hours," Rollison said. "No need to alarm the girl until then — just say he was hurt."

"She wants to come over at once."

"She'll be better off where she is," Rollison decided, then immediately changed his mind. "No. I'll talk to her here if you'd like to bring her over. Aunt —" He paused.

"What is it?"

"It happened just as she said it would."

"Of course it did," said Lady Hurst.

As she rang off, Rollison went tense again, hoping for a call from Olivia. It still did not come. By now he was aware of Clay watching him with revived suspicion, and the detective said:

"What's worrying you, Mr. Rollison?"

Rollison began to tell him, but before he finished Clay snapped his fingers at one of his men and said:

"You know Miss Cordman by sight, don't you? Red hair, five feet one —"

"I know her, sir."

"Go down to the car and have a general call put out for her — London and Home Counties. What was the car, Mr. Rollison? . . . A black Morris 1000, Registration 5X2151. Thank you . . . Look slippy," Clay added to his man, who hurried out and down the stairs.

As the door closed, the telephone bell rang.

For a reason he could not understand, Rollison hesitated before picking it up. He felt sure this must be Olivia, yet now that she had telephoned at last — if in fact this *was* she — he feared she had bad news. At last he snatched up the receiver.

"Rollison."

"Otherwise known as The Toff," a man said in a sneering voice. "You listen to me, Toff. Get off the star-gazer case and forget anything you found at Mrs. Abbott's flat. If you don't, then one of your pet star-gazers won't gaze at anything else any more. She'll be as dead as Mrs. Abbott."

15

PRISONER

Clay was whispering hoarsely: "What is it? Who is it?"

"Rolly, I feel such a fool," Olivia said into the telephone. "The last thing I wanted was to make things worse for you, but I have."

The man with her muttered something.

Olivia gave a sharp exclamation, and for a few moments Rollison could hear nothing but a confused jumble of sound. Then Olivia came back on the line. "Rolly, he probably means it, and I *would* hate to die. Really I would."

"You won't," said Rollison, with a confidence he was very far from feeling. "It's all right, Olivia, we'll get you. Where are you?"

She appeared to ignore his question. "How's Lucifer?"

"Lucifer?" said Rollison, puzzled. "Oh, he'll be okay." It wasn't like Olivia to waste time on irrelevancies, he thought. "But *you*, Olivia. *Where are you?*"

Still she ignored his question.

"Oh, dear. So they *did* kill him. Poor Lucifer. If he were still alive I'd say go and talk to him – but he was always such a *moaner —*"

The line went dead.

Clay said in a voice tense with anger:

"Why didn't you let me talk to her?"

"It wouldn't have been much good," Rollison said, absently.

Lucifer, he thought. Olivia had been trying to tell him that *Lucifer* would know where she was. What was it she had said? – "But he was always such a moaner . . ." Moaner? Moaner? Why, *Mona*! thought Rollison excitedly, *of course*. Olivia had been trying to tell him that he could get help from either Lucifer Stride or Mona Lister.

Clay was looking impatient. "Is she all right?"

"She's being held prisoner. I'm to get off the case."

"That wouldn't exactly make me cry," Clay said drily.

Rollison shrugged. "I may *have* to get off the case, but not yet. That man's accent was Rhodesian – Madam Melinska comes from —" Rollison stopped short.

"What is it?" Clay demanded in alarm.

"I meant to ask you to send someone to the Marigold Club, Madam Melinska and the girl —"

"You needn't worry about *them*," Clay said impatiently. "In view of what's happened you wouldn't expect us to let that pair roam about loose, would you? They'll be looked after. Did Miss Cordman give you any clue where she was being held prisoner?"

The question was whether to tell Clay or not. Once the police knew, they would want to take action, and Rollison was well aware that this might be disastrous. Any appearance on the scene by the police would not only tell the Rhodesian that he, Rollison, was not going to give up the case, but that he was working with the law. And yet —

Clay had surprisingly clear grey eyes, and a sensitive mouth in spite of his square face and massive chin. There was a pleasing quality in him, and quite suddenly it showed in his face and in his manner.

"Mr. Rollison," he said, "I *want* to help, you know. We've got off on the wrong foot and no doubt it's as much my fault as yours, but that doesn't matter now. I know you've often done a great deal on your own and — " he waved at the Trophy Wall — "*there's* the proof that it hasn't been a waste of time. But if you go off on a lone wolf act without consulting us, well, it does make things a bit difficult. But I'm as ready to listen to reason as Mr. Grice."

Rollison watched, listened, and warmed to this man; such a speech must have cost a considerable effort.

"She did give me a clue," he said simply. "Two clues. Lucifer Stride and Mona Lister could help us — presumably to find out where she is. Stride can't at the moment, so Mona will have to. Only —" he paused.

"She won't talk to the police?"

"I doubt it," Rollison agreed. "But I've just thought of something. Supposing I fooled these people into thinking I *would* do a deal and that I *would* give up Madam Melinska's defence. Only this would have to be another of my lone wolf acts." He smiled. "Once *you* had anything to do with it they'd know I was working with you."

Clay looked dubious. "But you've no assistance to

call on – apart from us. Your East End pals won't play, Jolly's in no condition to help, so if we weren't in on it you'd be entirely on your own."

Rollison shrugged. "It's the only chance we've got. Clay, all you need do is let me have my head. Or close your eyes when I slip away."

Clay grunted. There was no reason to expect him to commit himself, and Rollison dropped the subject until, ten minutes later, Lady Hurst, Madam Melinska and Mona arrived.

Clay was hearty.

"Time I went, Mr. Rollison. Hope you have a quiet night." He disappeared down the stairs.

"I don't know whether I like or dislike that man," Lady Hurst said, as Rollison led his guests into the living-room. "I don't think I would trust him too far."

"Never mind *him*!" said Mona. "Is there any news from the hospital?"

"Not yet," Rollison said gently.

"Oh, it's awful!" Mona cried. Her eyes were closed, now. "I hate it, *I hate it*. Being able to see what's happening to people and not being able to help." She shivered. "I know he's lying very still, there are people in white all about him, it's an operating theatre, I'm sure of that. But I can't see his face, I know he's there but I can't *see*!" She began to scream.

Rollison thought, there's only one way to get her out of this, *smack* her out of it. As the thought entered his head, Madam Melinska got up very deliberately, went across to the girl and slapped her on each side of the face.

Mona's eyes opened and she stopped screaming.

"She will be very tired now," Madam Melinska re-marked calmly. "But we should not leave her alone. If you could get some coffee —"

"Mona," Rollison said sharply, "how long have you known Lucifer Stride?"

She gaped at him.

"Tell me — how long?"

"Why — why, we only met today. We —"

"Don't lie to me."

"But it's true!"

"You met him only this morning and you're almost off your head with anxiety for him now. Tell me the truth."

The girl said desperately: "It is true. We only met today."

"How long have you known Lucifer Stride?" Rolli-son thundered.

The girl's lips quivered, her whole body shook. Lady Hurst glanced anxiously at Madam Melinska, who kept a hand on the girl's arm but did not interfere. Rollison leaned forward, accusingly, anger showing in his eyes and echoing in his voice.

"How many more are going to die before you tell the truth? *He* might die."

"Oh, no. No!" Terror flared up in her. "He mustn't, he mustn't die."

"*How long have you known him?*"

The girl closed her eyes and began to rock to and fro, to and fro, as if in an orgy of grief.

"Richard —" began Lady Hurst.

"*Quiet!*"

"Mona, my child," Madam Melinska interpolated, "you must tell all the truth. Lying won't help you or your friends any more. It won't help Lucifer and it can greatly hurt you. What *is* the truth?"

"I hate you, I hate you, I hate everyone!" Mona cried. "I can't help it if I can *see* what's going on somewhere else, I wish I couldn't, I don't want to, don't you understand, I don't want to!" Tears began to spill from her closed eyes, but the body tension had eased. "I — I've known him for years. He — he came to Rhodesia to visit his brother, Mick — Mick Fraser."

Madam Melinska glanced at Rollison and then asked the question which he was about to put. "Where does he live, Mona? Have you been to see him?"

"Ye — yes, I have. And I'm grown up, no one can tell me what I can do or what I can't. Where I go is nothing to do with anybody."

"Of course it isn't," said Madam Melinska soothingly, "no one's going to stop you seeing him. Where does he live, child?"

"He — he — he has a flat in Hampstead."

"What is the address?" Rollison asked sharply.

Lucifer and Mona, he thought. Lucifer and Mona. If he had read Olivia's message correctly, she had been trying to tell him that both Lucifer and Mona knew where she was held prisoner. Could this be in Stride's flat?

"It — it doesn't matter —"

"Mr. Rollison only wants to help him," said Madam Melinska.

"He's in hospital—only the doctors can help him now."

Rollison stood up abruptly.

"It's no use," he said. "I'll have to get on to the police."

"Police?" echoed Madam Melinska.

"They'll be able to find out where he lives. In fact it might be better if they had a look round instead of me. I must hurry," Rollison added, and turned towards the door, wondering whether such a transparent ruse could possibly work. He was halfway across the room when Mona sprang from the couch and rushed at him, snatching his arm, pulling him round, beating at his chest and face.

"I'll kill you; I won't let you go to the police, I'll kill you!"

He fended her off, gripping her wrists.

"If you give me Lucifer's address then I won't have to go to the police," he said.

"Why do you want it?" she screamed.

"I want to learn all I can about Lucifer Stride. Mona, if I find anything bad —"

"*There isn't anything bad!*"

" — I'll come back here and tell you, then we can both decide what to do about it," he said gently.

She stood silent, and he let her go. Her arms dropped to her sides, all the fight gone out of her; but her fear was very deep. She moved away a little, and then said:

"It's 5 Hill Crescent Road. The house is divided into four flats. His is upstairs—Flat A. But you won't find anything bad."

Obviously she was terrified in case she was wrong, thought Rollison; and she would not feel so keenly unless she had reason to fear that she might be.

Rollison pulled the Bentley up in Hill Crescent, from which led Hill Crescent Road. Outside, the calmness of the night was in strange contrast to what had happened before. Cars were parked at intervals, here and there a light glowed at a window, and the street lamps were alight but strangely remote.

Rollison approached Hill Crescent Road.

Not far away was the dark silence of Hampstead Heath; in the distance, a glow in the sky from London's West End, where the lights would soon begin to dim, for it was past midnight. Rollison, wearing rubber-soled shoes, reached the iron gate which led to Number 5. It squeaked as he opened it. A porch light glowed softly, but all the windows were in darkness. He closed the gate gently, stepped to the right, off gravel and on to grass, and approached the front door.

No one stirred.

Taking a pencil torch from his pocket, he shone it on to the lock. It was a straightforward Yale and easy to force, and in a few moments he was standing in the hallway.

A flight of carpeted stairs led upwards to a small landing, and Rollison crept towards it. Soon he was standing outside a door beneath which shone a narrow band of light.

This was Flat A.

16

SPELL-BINDER

Somewhere in the flat across the landing, faint music came from radio or record-player. Apart from this there was silence. Rollison examined the lock, and found that this also could be forced without difficulty. Very soon the door was open and he found himself in a small, brightly-lit hall, from which led four doors.

A voice sounded in the room straight ahead, and for a moment Rollison stood still – then he breathed a sigh of relief. His hunch had paid off. It was the voice of Olivia Cordman.

" . . . you're both utterly wrong. Madam Melinska is probably the best seer in the world – certainly she's the most famous —"

"*In*famous, you mean." A man's voice this time, and Rollison at once recognised it as that of the man who had telephoned him.

"That's not true." Olivia sounded angry. "If *you* knew what *I* know about her —"

"And if *you* knew what *we* know about her. All this second-sight and fortune-telling nonsense, it's the biggest racket out."

Rollison started. Surely that was the voice of the man who had held him up on the staircase at Gresham Terrace. Very gently, very quietly, he pushed the door open.

Olivia was sitting tied to a high-backed chair. The two men were watching her, their backs to the door.

"Pity *you* don't have second sight," said Rollison easily, "or you might have seen me coming."

Both men swung round to face him.

There was just time for Rollison to see that one of them was indeed the man who had threatened him on the stairs, then to notice, with a start of surprise, the strong physical resemblance between them, before they sprang at him, their reflexes so perfectly in tune that they both moved at the same instant. He had anticipated what they would do and was ready for them; and hatred of what they had already done added power to the blow he rammed into one man's jaw, the kick he landed on the other's stomach. As they staggered back he went for them with a fury which almost frightened him, drawing back only when one lay in a crumpled heap on the floor and the other was draped across a chair. Rollison, breathing hard, brushed his hair back and smiled at Olivia.

"Aren't you going to untie me?" she asked.

"Aren't I going —"

"I thought you always moved *fast*."

He saw her mischievous smile, chuckled, then took a pen-knife from his pocket and cut the rope which bound her. "Have they hurt you?" he asked gently.

"No. But I do feel a bit tottery." She stood up gingerly and almost collapsed; Rollison grabbed her and she leaned against him. "Rolly dear, am I glad to see you! What are you going to do with them?"

"Hand them over to the police. What else?"

"Sure they wouldn't talk more freely to you?"

"If you mean will I do a deal with your two nice young friends, the answer is no," Rollison said flatly.

"You could pretend to."

"There's no need, now that you're free."

"What do you mean, there's no need?" she demanded. "Catching *them*'s not the main job, clearing Madam Melinska is. *Have* you cleared her yet?"

"No, but —"

"There isn't any 'but' about it, until she's proved innocent you can pretend anything, you don't have to play by the Queensberry Rules with *that* lot." She seemed angrier with Rollison than with her abductors. "If you hand them over to the police they'll only tell them all about that beastly old dossier, and that won't do Madam Melinska any good at all — oh yes, they know all about it, Lord knows how, but they do. And once the police get on to *that*, Madam Melinska won't stand a chance."

Rollison said slowly: "I don't think she will."

"There you are then!" Olivia was triumphant. "*You've* got to make them talk. And if you can't, I can — everyone talks to me when I set my mind to it."

"That I can believe," said Rollison. He chuckled as he looked down at her. "You take some beating!"

"You're not so bad yourself. I thought you'd tumble to what I meant when I talked about Lucy being a moaner. How is he?"

Rollison told her the latest news about Lucifer

Stride. Then he turned towards the two men. The man who had threatened him on the stairs still sprawled across the chair, motionless; but the man who had telephoned him was beginning to stir.

Rollison leaned over him. "I'll take this one first. Any idea who they are?"

"That one's Bob. The other's Frank. Or that's what they called themselves. They didn't tell me any more —except that they're brothers."

Rollison pulled the man to his feet.

"Don't worry, we'll soon find out all we want to know. Got that famous reporter's biro of yours? I'd like you to take down what they say."

Olivia rummaged in a sideboard, found pencil and paper, and sat down, crossing her legs. "Okay, Rolly, I'm all set."

Bob was moistening his lips.

"What's your name?" demanded Rollison.

"Webb. Robert Webb."

"Where are you from?"

"Bul — Bulawayo, Rhodesia."

"What work do you do?"

Robert Webb hesitated. "I — we —"

"Just answer for yourself."

"I'm — I'm a private inquiry agent."

"You're a *what*?"

"I'm a private inquiry agent."

"You won't be any more," Rollison said grimly. "What work have you been doing?"

"Finding — finding out about Madam Melinska."

"Did *you* prepare that dossier?"

"I – er – we – yes."

"Who paid you?"

"Mrs. – Mrs. Abbott."

"Why did you go to her flat to steal the report you yourself had prepared and given to her?" This was a shot in the dark, but Rollison hoped it might pay off.

"I didn't steal it."

"You went to Tillson Street and broke into her flat. While you were looking for the report she returned unexpectedly, and you killed her."

"I *didn't* kill her!"

"*And* you killed Charlie Wray, a harmless little man who —"

"I didn't kill *anyone*!"

"You ran him down."

"That – that wasn't my fault, he ran right into my car."

"Oh-ho, so you *did* go to Tillson Street." Rollison's shot in the dark *had* paid off. "And this evening you followed me from Gresham Terrace and tried to run *me* down on the Embankment."

"I never ran you down."

Rollison moved forward and gripped Robert Webb's lapels, drawing him close. He could feel the man trembling, sensed the depth of his fear. He held him for several seconds, then thrust him away. Webb staggered backwards, stumbling against the far wall.

"I tell you I didn't run you down!"

"You're lying," Rollison said ominously.

"I'm not lying. I wasn't on the Embankment tonight."

"Perhaps you didn't kidnap Miss Cordman."

"Of course I did! I'd been to your flat to see what had happened to my brother. When I got there, your man was unconscious, and Lucy – Lucifer Stride – looked as if he were dead. Frank was just coming round. I managed to get him downstairs and into the car, and then *she* – " he nodded towards Olivia – "began to follow me. I didn't —"

He was interrupted by a groan from his brother.

Rollison turned to Olivia.

"I'm going to tie Frank to the chair," he said. "I want you to get a detailed statement from him. I'll take his brother in the next room and get one from him. If their stories tally, there may be some truth in what they're saying. If they don't —"

"They will!" gasped Bob Webb. "They will, I swear it."

The two statements tallied in practically every detail. The brothers were private inquiry agents, they had been employed by Mrs. Abbott to get information regarding Madam Melinska, they had got the information statement by statement, they had compiled the dossier and had brought it to her in London. Bob had been to see her that afternoon, not to get the dossier back but to give her further information. And he swore that she had been alive when he left.

Once Mrs. Abbott had realised that Rollison was going to help Madam Melinska, she had bribed the brothers to help her frighten him off. Bob had made the ammonia bomb which Mrs. Abbott had thrown at him screaming that she wanted to kill him. Frank had threatened him on the staircase of his flat. When Jolly had locked him in the bathroom he had, as Rollison had suspected, taken morphia so as to be proof against questioning. Both brothers admitted carrying morphia — they sometimes smuggled political prisoners over various borders in Southern Africa, said Frank, and morphia kept their charges quiet. He had come round to find both Jolly and Lucifer Stride unconscious, and a few minutes later his brother arrived and helped him downstairs and into the car, and they had driven straight here.

"But why here?" Rollison had asked sharply. "This is Lucifer Stride's flat. What connection have you got with Stride?"

"Stride's flat be damned," Bob had exclaimed. "It's ours. Stride was only staying with us. He's been working for us. We paid him to get information about Madam Melinska from the girl — Mona Lister."

17

CLEAN SWEEP

"The problem is, what are we going to do about the Webbs?" Olivia demanded. "I don't think —"

She was interrupted by a heavy knock at the front door, followed by a long, loud ring.

"It looks as if we don't have to make a decision," Rollison said.

"What do you mean?"

"Only the police would make such a din," Rollison told her, and opened the living-room door as a man called out in a deep but clear voice:

"Open, in the name of the law!"

"Coming!" Rollison moved towards the front door and opened it on three men, one of them Clay. He stepped aside and two of them pushed past, while Clay stayed with him.

"We know Miss Cordman's here," said Clay. "One of our boys saw the Morris in the drive."

"Perceptive of you."

"*And* the Webbs."

"So you know who they are," sighed Rollison.

"We had a long cable from Bulawayo," said Clay

with obvious satisfaction. "We know what they've been doing — *and* we know how well they succeeded. We took the opportunity of visiting Miss Cordman's apartment — just in case she had been attacked there."

"Oh," said Rollison, his heart dropping.

"What's that you said?" demanded Olivia, coming out of the living-room. "You went to my apartment?"

"And found the reports on Madam Melinska," announced Clay with heavy satisfaction. "I'd like to know where you got those, Miss."

Rollison answered for her, telling Clay the story of his visit to the Space Age Publishing offices. As he finished, the two brothers slouched into the hallway, each handcuffed to a detective.

"We only did our job," blustered Frank, "*we* didn't kill anybody, Inspector — straight up we didn't."

Bob was more truculent.

"*He's* the guy who's caused all the trouble." He nodded towards Rollison. "Just like the bloody police to pick on us. *We've* done nothing. Why don't you arrest *him*?"

"That'll do," said Clay sharply. He nodded to the detectives. "Take them to Cannon Row, I'll be over soon."

The men went out, leaving Olivia, Rollison and Clay alone. Clay turned to Rollison. "Found out what Stride was up to?" he demanded.

"According to the Webbs, he was using Mona Lister to get information about Madam Melinska — for which the Webbs paid him."

Clay pursed his lips.

"Sounds a bit far-fetched to me. Would the girl be *likely* to betray her accomplice? She must have realised that if Madam Melinska ended up in the dock, she'd end up in the dock with her — as she has done. There's more in this than meets the eye." He studied Olivia thoughtfully. "What do *you* think about it all, Miss Cordman?"

"What do *I* think? I think the whole thing's ridiculous. Why the police want to bring this absurd charge against Madam Melinska I can't imagine. She'll be acquitted, of course," added Olivia, with well-assumed confidence, "and *then* you'll all look pretty silly, won't you?"

Clay said drily: "From what I've seen from those reports, she'll get seven years at least."

Olivia gasped. "Oh, *no!*" She swung round to face Rollison, seizing his hand. "You've got to save her. You've *got* to, it will be a tragedy if you don't."

"For you and *The Day* because you've sponsored her?" asked Rollison mildly.

"Rolly, you are a beast. She must be innocent. She *must* be."

Very slowly, Rollison said: "I certainly hope so, Olivia."

There was a moment's silence. Then Olivia passed a weary hand over her forehead.

"But what about the *murder*? What about the attack on *you* on the Embankment? What about the attacks on Lucifer and Jolly? If the Webbs weren't responsible, then who was?"

"Let's make quite sure that the Webbs *weren't*

responsible," Clay said smugly. "And now there's no need for us to keep either you or Mr. Rollison any longer.

Rollison smiled. "Thank you, Inspector. My car's just round the corner, but I don't expect Miss Cordman feels much like driving, so I'd be grateful if someone could run the Morris back for me."

Clay nodded, and taking Olivia's arm, Rollison ushered her out of the flat and led the way downstairs.

Several policemen were stationed outside Number 5, but no one was near the Bentley.

Rollison saw Olivia in, then got in himself and took the wheel. She sat very still and was uncharacteristically silent as he drove. There was little traffic going in the London direction, but a lot coming towards them.

"Clay will be good when he's had more experience," Rollison said.

Olivia sniffed.

"I won't be sorry to get some sleep," he added, pulling up at the traffic lights at Swiss Cottage. Olivia sniffed again, and glancing down, he saw that she was crying, big tears rolling down her cheeks. "Hey, hey!" Rollison protested, with the embarrassment of seeing a woman cry. "It isn't as bad as that!"

Through her tears, Olivia said: "Yes, it is."

"But surely —"

"You don't understand at all!" cried Olivia. "Tens of thousands, hundreds of thousands of women *believe* in Madam Melinska. Unhappy women, ageing women, women with no hope, no purpose, no will to go on living. And she's given them that hope, that purpose, that will. What do you think will happen to them if she's found guilty? Oh yes, I know —"

A car behind them hooted impatiently.

"The light's green!" ejaculated Rollison, and started off. The car behind roared past.

"— I know *you* think it's a lot of poppycock, but whether it is or it isn't—and it isn't, actually—doesn't matter. What matters is that all these people have faith in it. Most of them are simple, unsophisticated, *decent* people leading drab and dreary lives—they *need* this faith. You and that stuffy old establishment policeman think it's merely a question of whether one woman goes to prison for a few years, but it's much more than that. You don't even *begin* to understand."

Rollison pulled into the side of the road, which ran through Regent's Park, took a handkerchief from his pocket, and dabbed Olivia's cheeks. She took the hand-kerchief, dabbed more vigorously, and added:

"But don't think I'm not grateful for what you've done."

Rollison smiled gently.

"You're quite a person, Olivia," he said. "I'd no idea. I'll take you home, and in the morning we'll size up the situation and see what we can do."

"So long as you'll do something," she said gruffly. "I have to admit, I *am* tired." She smiled up through the drying tears, and added: "You're quite a person, too."

Half an hour later, he left her at Chelsea.

A quarter of an hour after that he reached Gresham Terrace, to find Jolly up and in a dressing-gown, but everyone else gone. Jolly looked more than his age, but seemed very relaxed and was obviously pleased to see Rollison.

" . . . Lady Hurst felt it wiser that they should all go back to the Marigold Club, sir, and of course they had police protection. I am sure there is no cause at all for alarm. Coffee, sir? Or tea? Or something stronger?"

"Tea," said Rollison, "and we'll talk in the morning."

"Very good, sir."

"Jolly."

"Yes, sir?"

"What happened tonight?"

"Lucifer Stride called, sir, to ask your opinion of Madam Melinska's chances of being proved innocent. While we were talking I heard the prisoner stirring in the spare room, and went to investigate – and as I went through the door I was attacked from behind. But not by Stride, sir."

"Can you be sure?"

"He uses a quite unmistakable perfume, sir. I feel quite certain I would have noticed it."

"So you don't know the attacker. Jolly, what do you think of Madam Melinska?"

Jolly looked upon him earnestly, obviously weighing his words with great care.

"If I may say so, sir, I think she is harbouring a viper in her bosom. I would not trust the young woman an inch, despite her quite remarkable gifts. Apart from that – we *did* agree that we might be aptly described as anachronisms, didn't we, sir?"

"We did."

"At the risk of appearing to be old-fashioned, sir — my impression is that Madam Melinska is a very *good* person, quite incapable of deceit or trickery, fraud or dishonesty of any kind. It is an opinion which your aunt shares fully. In fact, sir, Lady Hurst will be deeply distressed and — ah — displeased if you are not able to establish Madam Melinska's innocence."

Rollison lifted his brows quizzically.

"Even if she is guilty?"

"I don't think Lady Hurst *or* I consider it a possibility that she is guilty, sir." After a pause, Jolly asked: "Will you have your tea here, sir, or in your room?"

"In my room," said Rollison, faintly.

Rollison woke to an unusual sound at this hour; men's voices. First Jolly's, then the voices of strangers, one deep and somehow not English, the other native Cockney. Police? wondered Rollison. Ebbutt's men? Then he heard the man with the deep voice saying:

"I think that's the lot, sir."

"I certainly hope so." Jolly sounded unbelieving. "*Five* sacks, did you say?"

"S'right," the Cockney said. "Full to blinking overflowing, mate. S'long."

Heavy footsteps followed, and the front door closed. There was silence. Five *sacks*? What would come in sacks and astonish Jolly? Rollison got out of bed and pulled on a blue dressing-gown, then went to the door and peered out.

Jolly was saying in a baffled voice: "There must be a thousand in each."

A thousand what?

Rollison reached the door of the living-room and saw five postal sacks dumped near the desk. Letters, thought Rollison, startled. Jolly, in his shirt-sleeves, stood and stared gloomily at the sacks.

"Someone's written to us," Rollison remarked.

Jolly started and turned round.

"Good morning, sir. I didn't hear you. Yes, they have indeed."

"I wonder if these could be letters of encouragement from strangers rooting for Madam Melinska," mused Rollison. He untied one of the sacks and took out a handful of letters. "London, W.1 – London, S.E.7 – Guildford, Surrey – Amersham, Bucks – Isleworth, Middx. You try a few, Jolly." He sat at his desk and slit open the five letters, then unfolded the first; a cheque fell out, for three guineas. The letter read:

"With very best wishes for your success in defending Madam Melinska – a small contribution to the cost of her defence."

Rollison opened the next letter; it contained a postal order for five shillings. The attached note read:

"In defence of the truth."

Jolly said: "A cheque for two pounds, sir, from someone who signs himself 'Well-wisher,' and a money order for thirteen shillings and sixpence, with a long letter on writing-paper inscribed with the signs of the Zodiac."

"Open a few more," Rollison told him.

Ten minutes later he picked up a pile of cheques and money orders, and made a rough calculation. Jolly watched him intently.

"Fifty-seven in all, and a total not far short of a hundred pounds." Rollison announced. "And there are at least five thousand."

"*Ten* thousand, I would say, sir."

"Sav two hundred times our hundred pounds," Rollison said. "Jolly, it can't be!"

"If the average remains the same, there are twenty thousand pounds in those sacks." Jolly drew a hand across his forehead and went on in an unsteady voice: "I think I will go and make your tea, sir."

18

ONLY THE BEGINNING

"Why, it's absolutely marvellous!" cried Olivia, as she stared at the enormous piles of letters on Rollison's desk. Her eyes were radiant, her cheeks glowing. It was half past ten, and she had just arrived. Except for a dozen telephone calls, two abusive, the others from people promising support, there had been no new developments. Rollison was dressed and had breakfasted, Jolly had regained his composure but was a little subdued. "It's wonderful!" Olivia went on. "Look at them. *How* much so far?"

"Three hundred and one letters opened, and a total of five hundred and seventeen pounds, ten shillings and sixpence," answered Rollison. "We shall soon hear remarks about fools and their money."

"Not from you, I hope," Olivia said. "These people aren't fools, they're simply — well, believers. But Rolly, you and Jolly can't possibly deal with all of these." She motioned to the unopened sacks and then opened one which was still three-quarters full. "And it's only the beginning."

"Beginning?" echoed Rollison, startled.

"Of *course!*" Olivia's eyes danced. "Whenever we have a special competition or a mail-order special, we get a post like this on the first day, but the main post comes in during the next two or three days."

"Don't for heaven's sake tell Jolly," said Rollison wryly.

"As a matter of fact, sir," Jolly said, coming from the door, "I wondered whether in these circumstances Mr. Ebbutt's men might have a change of heart. Their—ah—wives might have some sympathy with Madam Melinska."

"But you *can't* let a lot of ex-prize-fighters do this kind of work," protested Olivia. "Rolly—do you know what?"

"What?"

"*The Day* is fully equipped to handle this sort of thing. Our record was fifty-three thousand competition entries in one day. We've nothing big on at the moment. I'm sure that our Mailing and Receiving Department would be glad to cope."

"And what a story for *The Day*," said Rollison drily.

"Exactly! It would be a sensation. And we wouldn't charge for opening and sorting everything," Olivia added ingenuously.

"Telephone your Mailing and Receiving Department, straight away," said Rollison.

Before he had finished speaking, the telephone was in her hand. As she waited, there was a ring at the door, and Jolly moved towards it. At the same moment the unlisted telephone rang. Olivia talked, Rollison talked, Jolly and an unseen man talked at the door.

Rollison's caller was Roger Kemp, his solicitor.

"Rolly, I've been through all the papers I've got, all the reports I've heard, and I've been in touch with all my contacts at the Yard, *and* I've talked with counsel. Your Madam Melinska hasn't a chance in a million."

On the other telephone, Olivia was beaming with delight.

"Not one in a million," echoed Rollison, his heart dropping.

"She might get a reduced sentence if we plead that she was in a trance and unaware of what she was saying, but we would have to convince a jury that she really does go into these trances and there are a lot of people who simply wouldn't buy it."

"*Wonderful!*" Olivia was saying, ecstatically.

"And that's the best you can do?" asked Rollison lugubriously.

Jolly came in, carrying a thick wad of buff-coloured envelopes. Rollison saw but did not recognise them, thought "More letters," and heard Roger Kemp say:

"You *are* sure you want to go on with this aren't you?"

"Why shouldn't I be?"

"*Yes, send a van,*" cried Olivia. "And I'll come back on it."

"Up to you," the solicitor said, "but she could be fooling you. So far the one argument in her favour is that she appears to be nearly penniless. If that were proved to be untrue, then she would get a very stiff sentence for trading on the gullibility of the public and betraying trust. But you know that."

"How long?"

"I'd guess seven years."

"*Seven years!*" echoed Rollison.

Olivia replaced her receiver and came towards Rollison, but at the sight of his expression, the sound of his "*Seven years!*" she stood stock still.

" . . . so be absolutely sure of yourself," the solicitor said. "May I make a suggestion?"

"Go ahead."

"Let me arrange a meeting between you, Madam Melinska and counsel."

"I'll think about it," Rollison said. "Thanks, Roger." He rang off, and looked into Olivia's troubled eyes. "The law doesn't share anyone's faith," he said. "Like Clay said, she could get seven years."

"It's — *impossible!*"

"It isn't, my dear. It's grimly possible."

Olivia was silent for a long time; then, suddenly, her face cleared and she gave a bright little laugh.

"It isn't going to happen — *you're* going to save her. Rolly, it's all arranged, *The Day*'s sending a van and two men, you and Jolly won't have to do a thing, and you can get the best counsel in all England with *this* money. My, what a story this is going to be! You needn't worry, I *know* it's going to be all right!" She flung her arms round him and gave him a hug.

"Excuse me, sir," said Jolly.

"*More* letters?"

"Telegrams, sir."

"Tele — good Lord!"

"Oh, they'll come by the hundred," Olivia declared.

"I tell you, you're only just beginning to understand what people think about Madam Melinska. And they're right, Rolly, you'll find out!" She hugged him again, and asked in the same breath: "What shall we do with the money? Open a Madam Melinska Defence Account with it?"

Rollison said slowly: "No. Just a Madam Melinska Account."

"Rolly, *she* won't touch the money."

"That's good," said Rollison.

"You still doubt her, don't you?" Olivia said. "I — what's that?" She ran to the window and looked out. "It's the van! I'll go and let the men in!"

Before Jolly could open the door she reached it and went bounding down the stairs. As she did so, the unlisted telephone bell rang again.

Rollison lifted the receiver.

"It's the telephone answering service, Mr. Rollison," a girl said. "There are several calls which I really think you ought to make — two to the B.B.C. about appearing on a news programme tonight, and *three* from Independent Television. I've a note of the people concerned, if —"

"Just tell them I'm very sorry," Rollison said.

"You don't want to appear on television?"

"Not tonight," Rollison said. "How are the other calls coming in?"

"We've two operators doing nothing else," the girl said. "And all except a few are wishing you luck."

"What about the few?"

"Abusive, sir, but nothing to worry about — not

everyone believes in Madam Melinska, I'm afraid." The girl laughed. "You're sure about the television?"

"Positive," said Rollison firmly.

He rang off as Olivia and two youths came upstairs for the mailbags. As she went out, shooing the youths before her, she called:

"Rolly, I keep meaning to find out how Lucifer is. *Do* ring the hospital."

He had completely forgotten Lucifer Stride.

"He is doing as well as can be expected, sir."

"Is he out of danger?"

"No, but every hour improves his chances."

"Good. Has he had any visitors?"

"The police are at his bedside, sir."

"Ah, yes. They would be. Thank you."

"Is Chief Inspector Clay in, please."

"One moment, sir —"

"Clay speaking."

"Rollison here. How are you this morning?"

"Very well, sir, thank you. How are you?"

"Coping with many thousands of gifts for Madam Melinska's defence."

"*Thousands?*"

"*Many* thousands."

"Really, sir — they always say there's one born every minute!"

"Yes. Have the Webbs talked?"

"They haven't changed their story in any degree at all."

"Believe them?"

"That's not for me to say."

"No, I suppose not. Clay."

"Yes, sir?"

"Have you talked to Michael Fraser, Edward Jackson and Jane somebody at the Space Age Publishing offices?"

"I have, sir. And they confirm your story."

"I'm delighted to hear it," said Rollison drily. "Tell me – do you think *they* could have tried to run me down? And attacked Lucifer Stride?"

"Not as far as I know, sir. I've checked their movements very closely."

"Could they have murdered Mrs. Abbott?"

"The man Jackson admits he was in Mrs. Abbott's flat and that he took away the file on Madam Melinska, but *if* what Fraser and the girl say is correct, then he was back at the office with the file before Mrs. Abbott was killed."

"He was, was he? Going to charge him?"

"No decision has been reached, sir."

"You're commendably cautious. Chief Inspector —"

"Yes, sir?"

"Have you found out whether Madam Melinska has in fact substantial funds?"

"Not yet, sir."

"If you find that she has, this will be evidence against her, won't it?"

"*Added* evidence, sir."

"Thank you, Clay, thank you very much; you're being most helpful."

"Thank *you*, sir."

"Jolly."

"Yes, sir."

"*Could* anyone have known that we were on the threshold of our fiftieth case?"

"I've found no evidence to show that they could, sir. I've checked with three of the most attentive newspapers and their files show under forty cases."

"So no one could have known."

"They could have guessed, sir."

"Or 'seen'?"

"I suppose it *is* conceivable, sir."

"Richard?"

"Why, hello, Aunt Gloria."

"It's nearly lunch-time, and I've been expecting you to telephone all the morning."

"I didn't want to disturb you, Aunt."

"There is no need for schoolboy sarcasm. I understand from Miss Cordman that a quite remarkable demonstration of public faith has been shown and that *eleven* thousand pounds have been subscribed for Madam Melinska's defence. She is deeply touched."

"It's a lot of money, Aunt. Do you think she might now be persuaded to say a word in her own defence?"

"Precisely what do you mean, Richard?"

"I'd like her to meet counsel."

"I do not believe she would refuse, but you must ask her yourself."

"I'll do that. How is Miss Lister?"

"The young woman appears to be greatly distressed."

"I'm not surprised. Aunt Gloria."

"Yes?"

"I noticed that she was wearing some nice-looking jewellery, a diamond brooch, ear-rings and bracelet."

"Your powers of observation were always reasonably good, Richard."

"Thank you, Aunt. How are yours?"

"Are you asking me whether the diamonds are real?"

"Yes."

"They are."

"Three thousand pounds' worth of real, would you say?"

"Approximately, yes."

"Well, well. Thank you very much, Aunt."

"Mr. Richard Rollison?"

"Speaking?"

"Your call to Bulawayo, Rhodesia, Mr. Rollison."

"Thank you . . . Hallo, Bill. How are you?"

"Very well, old boy. Suspicious of you, though. Why this sudden call from the dear old homeland?"

"A rich banker like you must be used to such calls. Could you do me an unlawful favour?"

"It depends."

"You've doubtless heard of Miss Mona Lister."

"I have indeed."

"Is she rich? And have certain fairly substantial sums of money been credited to her account recently? . . . Wait a moment, Bill. I've air-mailed you a list of the amounts concerned. If you could check it or have it checked —"

"Quite impossible, old boy. No banker can divulge a client's private affairs except to the police."

"I know. But if you return my list with credits she *hasn't* received crossed off, and those she *has* received in all their virgin freshness, I can deduce as necessary, can't I?"

"Richard, you are a cunning so-and-so."

"No doubt."

"I make no promises."

"Tell me one thing."

"If it's not divulging private and confidential information, I will."

"Have the police asked to see Mona Lister's account?"

"No. They haven't asked me not to answer any questions about her, either."

"Bill, you're a devious fellow indeed."

"How like like to recognise like, Rolly! I'll be in touch."

"Soon, please. Just as soon as you can. I'll be *very* grateful."

19

ALMOST THE END

For two weeks Rollison waited.

He was not inactive. Letters still came in by the sackful, some enclosing a shilling or two, one a cheque for a hundred guineas, and the total of contributions rose by startling amounts daily. Every newspaper ran the story, and Rollison and Jolly were under almost constant siege.

"*How much more for Madam M.?*" asked the *Daily Globe*. "Already over thirty-one thousand pounds have been subscribed, an unsolicited tribute to the great faith that so many have in Madam Melinska and the mysteries of the influence of the stars."

"*How great a folly?*" demanded the solemn *Guard*. "It is almost unbelievable that in this day and age, some twenty thousand people should contribute to the defence of such a woman."

"*Can the Toff save Madam M.?*" cried the *Daily Record*.

And so the headlines ran, from day to day.

The Webbs, both charged with kidnapping, were remanded in custody. Rollison went to see them twice, but they did not change a word of their story.

Michael Fraser and Ted Jackson, of Space Age Publishing, sent Rollison the reports for which he had asked, but neither contained any information other than that which they had already given him.

Any faint hope of saving the company had now vanished. "The money just isn't there," said Michael Fraser.

A letter reached Rollison two days late because of the diversion of his post to *The Day*. It was from Bill Ebbutt.

"There's no more hard feelings down this way, Mr. R., but if you ask me, it would be better if you stayed away until this fortune-telling case is over. About two to one *against* Madam M. in these parts, I'd say."

Despite the many thousands of letters Rollison had received, this was probably representative of a good cross-section of the public.

"Oh, they're *crazy*," Olivia Cordman said. "You don't want any *more* proof that the woman's genuine, surely." She was working all day and most of the night making sure that every letter was answered individually.

"Rolly," said Roger over the telephone, "if you want counsel to appear for Madam Melinska at the Magistrates Court, he'll need briefing today. Normally counsel wouldn't appear at this stage, but Sir David Bartolph is interested — very interested. He's a bit of a clairvoyant himself, you know. A lot of queer rumours circulate about him. Madam Melinska couldn't do better and she could do a lot worse if she lets him go."

"If you really believe I should, Mr. Rollison, I will

certainly see this legal gentleman," said Madam Melinska.

At the time Rollison was telephoning Roger Kemp to tell him that Madam Melinska had agreed to see Sir David Bartolph, Chief Inspector Clay was in the small hospital ward where Lucifer Stride had just been taken off the danger list. Stride's face and hands were white as chalk, and he looked a sick man. Clay sat by his side, like a watching bulldog.

"Someone nearly killed you, Stride. This is their second attempt, isn't it? And if you let them get away with it, there may be a third. Third time lucky, so they say."

Stride moistened his lips, but said nothing.

"Who was it?" demanded Clay. "You won't help yourself by keeping quiet, you know." After a pause he went on: "Tell us the truth, there's a good chap, and we'll see that there *isn't* a third attempt – but it's got to be the *whole* truth," he added warningly.

Stride's eyes flickered towards him.

"Will you help Mona?" he whispered hoarsely. "It's not her fault, I – I made her do it. I wish to God I hadn't."

"We'll help her all we can," said Clay reassuringly. "Now, who attacked you? – and why?"

Slowly, hesitatingly, Lucifer Stride began to talk. And the more he talked, the happier Clay looked.

Sir David Bartolph was a tall, distinguished-looking man, solid rather than fat, with iron-grey hair brushed straight back from his forehead, powerful shoulders, and a deep, pleasing voice. Rollison had seen him in Court, where he could be terrifying, but had never actually met him. He shook hands, but was obviously much more interested in Madam Melinska. Roger Kemp, short, alert, immaculately dressed, watched her fascinatedly.

They sat in a semi-circle in front of Bartolph's desk.

"Madam Melinska, let me say at once that I have read all the information available, including a most lucid statement from Mr. Rollison —" he glanced approvingly at Rollison. "There is, of course, one somewhat damning factor — your own reluctance to admit that you recall what happened on any of these occasions."

Madam Melinska, wearing a wine-red gown, a purple and gold scarf hiding her black hair, sat in an easy chair. Now and again she moved a sandal-clad foot; apart from that she appeared to make no movement at all.

"Do you understand me?" Bartolph asked.

"Perfectly, Sir David, although I do not agree."

This man was a leading Queen's Counsel.

"Indeed?"

"I am not at all reluctant to admit anything — I simply have no recollection of what I say during these readings."

"You still persist in that contention."

"I always persist in the truth, Sir David."

Bartolph stared at her fixedly.

"Then can you give me your solemn assurance that your readings are genuine? Can you give me your solemn assurance that your knowledge of your clients, their lives, their families, knowledge which they take to be an example of your powers of clairvoyance, second sight, call it what you will—"Bartolph waved an impatient hand—"and by which they are so impressed that they are subsequently prepared to follow your advice regarding the disposal of, in some instances, very large sums of money—" Bartolph paused, as if to add weight to his words—"Madam Melinska, I repeat, can you give me your solemn assurance that this knowledge *is* the result of your powers of clairvoyance and that it has not been previously acquired with a view to winning the confidence of your clients?"

Madam Melinska met his gaze unflinchingly. "You have my solemn assurance, Sir David."

Bartolph looked unblinkingly into the dark, gipsy-like face of the woman sitting before him, noting, with dispassionate appraisal, the beautiful bones, the proud carriage.

"Madam Melinska," he said at last, "I have an important decision to make in the near future. It is a personal decision, and nothing to do with investing money or any problem arising from my profession. I would be grateful for any guidance you can give me."

Roger Kemp pursed his lips in a soundless whistle. Rollison stirred.

"I will gladly help if I can."

"May I know your fee in advance?"

"I charge no fee, Sir David. I do not believe it right to charge for an ability for which I am not responsible."

"That is very unusual, Madam Melinska. One usually exploits one's abilities to make a living."

"It is not my way," said Madam Melinska.

"How *do* you make your living?" asked Bartolph quietly.

"I live on gifts," Madam Melinska replied.

"Gifts given out of gratitude."

"Sometimes. And out of kindness."

"Some would say that you place the onus of the size of your fee on others — that it would be fairer if you did make a charge."

"That has often been said," agreed Madam Melinska calmly. "It has also often been said of priests and holy men that they place the responsibility of keeping themselves on others whereas it should be their own responsibility."

"Do you agree with that?"

"No," answered Madam Melinska. "They — like myself — have certain powers. The practising of these powers requires deep concentration. They cannot switch this concentration on and off as if they were machines. It is not easy to acquire or to maintain a calm mind, Sir David. It is not easy for a man to be holy if he must always harass himself over the things he needs for living."

"I think I understand," said Bartolph. After a pause, he went on: "Do you think you can help me?"

Madam Melinska stared at him for a long time, then said very quietly, "I will try."

"May we all be present?"

"As you wish. I shall close my eyes and clasp my

hands. I may ask you questions from time to time. If I
do, please answer very simply."

"Very well."

Rollison glanced across at Roger, almost uneasily.
The woman sat motionless for several minutes – gradually her head drooped forward until her chin was almost
at her breast. She seemed to be breathing more deeply,
as if she were already sleeping. Suddenly she began to
speak.

"I see young people, many young people, and one of
them is a boy, almost on the threshold of manhood, a
boy who is very like you. He is laughing and appears
gay, as do all the others, but he is not truly happy and
his gaze keeps straying to one of three young women
across the room from him. This young woman is
beautiful, very beautiful. She is tall and very dark. I do
not believe she is English – she has a look of the Southern European, and yet . . ." Madam Melinska paused,
and her hands seemed to press together more tightly.
"There is an unusual mixture of ethnic groups in this
room; some are Spanish – some are Mexican – some
are Negro. The young man is in considerable emotional
distress. He is facing an issue of great importance to
him."

She stopped; and began to rub her hands together
very swiftly, almost wringing them. When she spoke
again, it was slowly, and with even greater concentration than before.

"This – young – man – is – your – son. He is in South
America – and he is undecided whether to return to
England or whether to stay. His decision is dependent

on the girl. No, not only on the girl, he has to make a choice. A choice between loyalty to his father – to you – and love for this young woman."

Bartolph was studying her intently, his eyes narrowed to slits. He hardly seemed to be breathing.

"You wish to know whether you should, in his own best interests, compel your son to come home. You must not do this. You must allow him to choose for himself. There is no way you can be sure that your decision would be the right one. It must be *his* decision."

She stopped speaking, the movement of her hands ceased; soon she was breathing more freely. It was several minutes before she opened her eyes, and then it was as if she had awoken from a long, deep sleep.

"I hope I was able to help you," she said diffidently.

Bartolph was gazing into space, a far-away look in his eyes. "It – it's uncanny," he muttered. There was a moment's silence, then, as if making an almost physical effort, he answered her question.

"Madam –" he hesitated – "Madam Melinska, no one – *no one* – apart from myself and my son could have known what you have just told me. And you will never realise how great your help has been."

Rollison and Roger Kemp exchanged almost imperceptible glances. Roger let out a long, slow, almost painful breath.

Madam Melinska looked gravely across the desk at Bartolph, but said nothing.

Bartolph squared his shoulders.

"Madam Melinska, I will be glad to undertake your defence, although I must warn you that it will not be easy to persuade the jury that you are innocent of the charges." The barrister taking over from the man, thought Rollison. "But I will endeavour – " continued Bartolph, placing the fingertips of each hand meticulously together – "to convince them that any advice you gave was advice given without your conscious awareness. Now we have a very difficult problem." He looked at Rollison. "Whether to use this defence in the Magistrates Court, or whether to allow Madam Melinska to be committed for trial at the Assizes so that I can plead to a jury. If we fail to convince the magistrate at this hearing, I doubt whether we should find it easy to convince a jury later."

"What do you advise, sir?" asked Roger Kemp.

"On the whole – to allow committal, so that we have more time to prepare the defence."

"Please," interrupted Madam Melinska. "I think it would be much better if you were not to wait. If it is possible, I would like to return to Rhodesia next month."

"If you're committed for trial, it won't be."

"I am fully aware of the risk," Madam Melinska said quietly.

"That was incredible – absolutely incredible," Roger said to Rollison. "*Could* she have already known about this son in South America, do you think?"

Rollison shrugged his shoulders helplessly.

Madam Melinska had gone back to the Marigold Club by taxi, and Roger and Rollison had taken their leave of Bartolph and were now at Roger's office. Roger had a baffled, almost a dazed look, which told of the measure of his bewilderment.

Rollison frowned. "Bartolph knows that he hasn't an earthly, of course. He's sticking his neck out simply because she hit the nail on the head as regards his son. She certainly made a big impression there – I've never known a Q.C. plead in a Magistrates Court before." He stood up. "Oh well, if you *can* think up some new angle I'll be damned grateful. I'll leave you to it, I can see myself out."

As he moved towards the door, the telephone bell rang.

Roger lifted the receiver. "Who? Yes, he's here." He beckoned to Rollison. "Rolly, it's for you."

"Nice timing," said Rollison, and stepped back to take the receiver. "Hallo . . . Oh yes, Jolly . . . Has it, then!" He stiffened – Jolly had reported that an airmail letter had just arrived from his banking friend in Rhodesia. "Open it, will you, and read it out to me."

There was silence for a few moments. When Rollison spoke, his voice sounded heavy. "I see. Thanks." He rang off.

Roger sensed his concern. "What is it, Rolly? Bad news?"

"Mona Lister has had the money. The money that the Webbs said was paid to Madam Melinska. It's been paid into Mona Lister's account – every penny of it." Rollison paused for a moment, then looked at Roger very straightly as he added. "And Mona Lister is Madam Melinska's partner."

20

SECOND HEARING

Rollison walked from the sunlit Temple Gardens, heavy-hearted, then towards the Strand. It was only a step out of his way to visit the Space Age Publishing offices, and he turned towards them, remembering vividly what had followed his first visit here. He was almost surprised when Jane did not come out of the door, stand and stare at him, and then run back inside. As he reached it, however, it opened – and he waited for events to repeat themselves.

Instead, Chief Inspector Clay stepped into the passage, with Michael Fraser just behind him.

Rollison drew back.

Clay gave the broadest grin Rollison had seen on his big face.

"Good afternoon, Mr. Rollison. I was coming to see you. I've some news for you. Lucifer Stride has made a statement exonerating Mr. Fraser and his friends of the murder of Mrs. Abbott, and accusing Bob Webb."

"So the Webbs *were* lying," exclaimed Rollison.

"Well, it was their only chance to save themselves," remarked Clay, in the heartiest of moods. "Can't give you the details, but the Webbs weren't after the dossier, they were after jewels – apparently Mrs. Abbott had a great deal of jewellery lying around her flat, and the Webbs got wind of it."

He went almost gaily along the passage and Rollison watched him turn a corner, then followed Fraser into the inner office. Ted Jackson was standing with his back to the window.

"Did you hear that?" asked Fraser.

"Yes. Afternoon, Mr. Rollison. Sorry we gave you an unfriendly reception the other day – but we were just so mad at you for defending Madam Melinska. We got the crazy idea we might scare you into dropping the case. But I guess you got your own back." He passed an explanatory hand over his jaw.

"Forget it." Rollison sat down in an office chair of black plastic and bright tubular steel. "So you're in the clear regarding Mrs. Abbott."

"But still broke," gloomed Jackson. "Cigarette?"

"Thanks." Rollison lit up. "Clay was in a very expansive mood. Did he tell you anything else?"

"Only that my half-brother, Lucifer Stride, was also after the dossier," said Fraser. "It seems that he'd talked Mona into doing something she shouldn't – Clay didn't say what, but he *did* say she was put up to it by Stride – and they were anxious to find out if the Webbs had got on to it. So Lucifer moved in with the Webbs and pretended to be working with them against Madam Melinska – in fact, he was trying to find out exactly how much they knew about Mona. Just what she *has* been up to I don't know."

"I *think* I can tell you," said Rollison slowly. "How's

this? It seems that most of Madam Melinska's clients came to her with money worries. I understand that Mona was always present when Madam Melinska gave her readings, so she would hear whatever advice Madam Melinska gave. Supposing, whenever she advised her clients to make an investment, Mona told them they must make this investment through Madam Melinska, and then intercepted the money before Madam Melinska saw it."

There was a moment's pause.

"It's *possible*," said Jackson.

Fraser looked shaken. "You mean *Mona's* at the bottom of the whole thing, and *not* Madam Melinska. I *can't* believe —"

"I can," Jackson interrupted. "Sorry, Mike and all that, I know you're still fond of the girl, but you know how persuasive that half-brother of yours can be. And she's fallen for him hook, line and sinker." He turned to Rollison. "In which case Madam Melinska's in the clear. But you'll never prove it. If she was in one of her trances she wouldn't know *what* Mona told anyone, and Mona's not going to admit anything. And according to the Webbs' dossier they had the devil's own job getting any of the *clients* to give evidence. Wait a minute, though." He looked across at Rollison. "Wasn't your aunt —?"

Rollison interrupted him. "She was," he said grimly, "and I've just remembered something. She sent her cheque direct to Space Age Publishing, Limited, and *that* disappeared as well. Which rather makes nonsense of what I've been saying."

Jackson looked at Fraser. Fraser looked at the floor. For a few moments there was silence.

Then Fraser turned to Rollison. "I didn't want to tell you this, I didn't think it had any bearing on the case, but now I suppose I'll have to. You know that Lucifer once worked here?"

Rollison nodded.

"He used to be a nice enough boy, though he was always weak. Couldn't stick to anything and easily influenced. Well, I'm afraid he got into a bad set, and turned into the black sheep of the family. I gave him a job in the firm hoping he'd pull his socks up—but he didn't."

"Go on," said Rollison.

"Well, one day I discovered he'd been dipping into the till as it were. A great deal of company money had been finding its way into his pockets, and I dare say your aunt's cheque was part of it. That's another reason why we're broke. Oh well, it never rains but it pours."

"We didn't prosecute," added Ted. "After all, he *is* Mike's brother. And we didn't want that kind of publicity. But we've got it now," he went on gloomily. "*We're* the people associated in the public's mind with Madam Melinska's"—he corrected himself—"*Mona's* swindle. Oh, all right, Mike, *Lucy's* swindle. No one's going to invest with us now. If we could only keep going for another six months or so we might weather it —but what with Lucy helping himself so liberally, and now this, we haven't a hope." He looked at Fraser and shrugged helplessly. "Oh well, we did try." Then making a brave attempt at flippancy, he turned to Rollison.

"*You* haven't got thirty thousand pounds to spare, have you?"

Rollison stared at him, blankly.

"Damn it, can't a man make a joke?" demanded Jackson. "Pretty good effort in view of the state of the market."

"Wait!" cried Rollison. "Wait!" He sat staring at the two men as if he could see right through them, then said in a strained voice: "Get me Roger Kemp on the telephone, will you? His number is . . ." As he waited, he still stared and a new hope began to put fresh blood in his veins. "Roger? . . . Roger, what would happen if Madam Melinska *did* put the money into Space Age Publishing? . . . The police wouldn't have a case, then, would they . . .? You're quite sure? . . . Well, well, well!" He beamed up at Fraser and Jackson. "No, don't go. Roger, I told you about these people who've sent all this money for Madam Melinska's defence, there's no reason why she shouldn't invest it in Space Age Publishing, is there? . . . No legal reason why the money shouldn't be used that way? . . . Wonderful!"

He rang off.

Ted Jackson was at the door.

"Jane, call the works, tell 'em we're going on — fix the advertisements we cancelled. Yes, we can guarantee them, we're back in business!" He swung round.

Michael Fraser was gripping Rollison's hand.

"It's the nearest thing I've ever known to a miracle," he said. "I can't thank you enough."

"Don't try," said Rollison. "One condition — that once you're back on your feet, all the people who've subscribed get their money back – or equivalent shares in Space Age Publishing."

"Guaranteed!" cried Jackson. "Wait until the world hears about this."

"But the world mustn't hear," said Rollison firmly. "At least, not yet. I want this to be sprung in Court."

Olivia Cordman looked up from her office desk in a small room near High Holborn. Her spectacles gave her a touch of severity; here she was very much the editor. Rollison rounded the desk, took her hands, pulled her to her feet and kissed her.

"Rolly! I didn't know you felt like that!"

"That was just a 'thank you' kiss," said Rollison. "Here's one to say: 'You're the most perspicacious woman's feature editor in the world'."

It was several seconds before he let her go. When at last he released her, she drew back, breathless. "Rolly, you idiot, what on earth's all that about. Whatever's happened?"

Rollison told her.

There was not an inch to spare in Court on the morning of the second hearing, but this time Rollison sat on a bench behind Roger Kemp and Bartolph. In the public gallery Lady Hurst contrived to look as if she had enough room. The newspaper benches were over-flowing. When Nimmo came in, brisk and business-like as ever, the oak-panelled room was as crowded as the London Underground during the rush hour. Al-most as soon as Nimmo sat down, the door beneath the dock opened and first Madam Melinska and then Mona appeared. The formalities were over in almost record time.

"How do the defendants plead?"

"Not guilty, your honour," said Sir David Bartolph. "With your permission, sir, I would like to submit evidence forthwith and to plead that there is no case to answer."

Nimmo looked across at Clay, sitting with the Public Prosecutor's solicitor.

"What have the police to say?"

"We have *more* than enough evidence to justify asking for a committal for trial," the Public Prosecutor's man said, while Clay looked almost smug.

Nimmo darted a glance from one to the other. "I'm quite sure you wouldn't waste the Court's time, Sir David."

"Thank you, your honour. I shall most certainly try not to. The facts of this case are simple. The accused are charged with misleading investors about the value of shares in a company known as Space Age Publishing, Limited, and also with misappropriating money paid for the shares bought on their advice. I herewith submit two facts and, if you wish, can produce witnesses to testify. First, that capital representing the full face value of the shares under discussion has been placed at the disposal of Space Age Publishing, Limited, by Madam Melinska. Second, that the orders received by Space Age Publishing, Limited are more than sufficient to ensure a profitable trading year and the payment of a dividend which will be guaranteed.

In view of these facts I do not think there is a case to answer."

Sir David Bartolph sat down.

Rollison had heard him and taken everything in, but had hardly seen him, for Madam Melinska's eyes were turned towards him, Rollison, and there was such benignity in them, such gratitude, that he could not look away.

Suddenly it dawned on him that the Court was in an uproar.

Over on the Press benches, Olivia Cordman was jumping up and down excitedly. The crowded public benches were a mass of laughing, waving women. As the news spread, the queues of people stretching for nearly half a mile in each direction began to cheer; the police were helpless, traffic jammed and stayed jammed, and it seemed as if the cheering would never stop.

It was three hours before it was safe for Madam Melinska, Mona and Rollison to venture out, and Lady Hurst was waiting at the Marigold Club when they arrived.

"I must say I am very pleased with you, Richard," she said. "It was highly gratifying. Don't you agree, Madam Melinska?"

"I do indeed," Madam Melinska said, taking Rollison's hands in hers. "Mr. Rollison, you will never really believe in your heart, you will always have doubts, and this is *you*, and I would not have it otherwise. Yet you are a man of great faith. What other man would attempt so often those tasks which the world believes are impossible?"

She paused, then drew him forward and kissed him on either cheek.

Rollison's aunt wiped away what looked remarkably like a tear.

"And now there's nothing left for you to do," said Olivia gaily.

Rollison looked across a dining-table at the Savoy Grill, where she sat happy and slightly flushed with wine.

"Don't you believe it," he said. "Now that I'm on the board of Space Age Publishing I have to make sure that all those little people get full value for their money. I had a talk with Mona, by the way. As Jackson thought, the girl was completely infatuated with Stride, and prepared to do anything he asked. It was he who thought up this little investment racket, and so under his thumb was she that she agreed. But she's come to her senses at last — and given Michael Fraser a cheque for every penny of the money she had from Madam Melinska's clients."

"So they'll get their investments in Space Age Publishing after all," said Olivia. "And Mike will get the investment money as well as Madam Melinska's defence money. That ought to put him back on his feet." Suddenly she looked grave. "But poor Mr. Abbott — if it hadn't been for Mona he would never —"

Rollison interrupted her. "It wasn't because of the money he lost that Abbott committed suicide. He'd plenty to spare. After all, he left his wife pretty comfortably off, didn't he — especially judging by all that jewellery the Webb brothers had their eye on. I've been having another chat with Michael Fraser — he used to be engaged to Mona and knew the family pretty well — and he says that Mrs. Abbott's possessiveness grew and grew until it was almost a disease. Abbott felt he just couldn't stand it any longer. And you remember — " Rollison looked across at Olivia — "it was this same possessiveness that drove Mona away from home."

"But Mrs. Abbott told us —"

Rollison raised a quizzical eyebrow. "Oh yes, she *told* us he'd killed himself because of the money he'd lost — in point of fact I think she'd fooled herself into really believing it, just like she'd fooled herself into believing that Madam Melinska had come between her and Mona — but this was because she simply couldn't face up to the truth."

"So she built up a great big hate against Madam Melinska and paid the Webbs to dig up anything they could that would reflect against her?" asked Olivia.

"She did. But it was Lucifer Stride's little scheme for making easy money that the Webbs dug up — although they didn't know that it was Stride's scheme. In Mrs. Abbott's favour, all the evidence *did* point to Madam Melinska's guilt."

"She should have known Madam Melinska wouldn't do such a thing," said Olivia flatly. "*I* knew. But there's still an awful lot unexplained. Who tried to run Lucifer Stride down outside your flat? Who tried to run *you* down? Who murdered Mrs. Abbott? Who attacked Lucifer and Jolly —?"

"Easy, easy," teased Rollison. "Not so many questions at once."

"—the night I was kidnapped," finished Olivia. "Don't be a beast, Rolly. You know I'm dying to hear."

Rollison laughed at her eagerness. "Okay, I'll tell you. Four answers in one. The Webb brothers. You remember that Stride was pretending to work with them in order to find out if they'd discovered that it was Mona, and not Madam Melinska, who'd stolen the investment money?"

Olivia nodded.

"Well, the Webbs hadn't found out about Mona—but they *did* find out that Stride was spying on them. They didn't know what information he was after and they didn't know whether or not he'd got it, but as they'd been pretty bad boys one way and another they got thoroughly rattled and thought they'd better dispose of him. Their first attempt was when they tried to run him down in Gresham Terrace—the second was when Bob came to rescue his brother from the flat, and found Stride talking to Jolly."

Olivia frowned. "What about the attack on you?"

"Once the Webbs had got all the information they could get regarding Madam Melinska, their job was finished. Mrs. Abbott had stopped paying them, and they were a bit pushed for cash—so, knowing about the jewellery, they decided to break into her flat and help themselves. Mrs. Abbott came back unexpectedly, one of the brothers panicked and strangled her, and they both took to their heels—" Rollison's voice hardened—"running down Charlie Wray in the process. When they were back at 5 Hill Crescent Road, Bob discovered that he'd dropped his wallet. Afraid he'd left it at the flat, he came back to look for it, but couldn't find it – panicked still further, and decided to burn the place down."

"Did he drop it at the flat?" asked Olivia.

"He did indeed. According to Clay, the ambulance men found it on the bed underneath the body. It must have fallen there during the struggle. And lucky it was that it did," added Rollison, "it was only when the police finally identified this wallet that the brothers broke down and decided to tell the truth."

"But *you*," urged Olivia. "Why did they attack *you*?"

"Well – " Rollison sipped his wine – "as Bob Webb left Mrs. Abbott's flat for the second time, he saw me arrive – then, half an hour later, the police. Talking it over, the two brothers convinced themselves that, during that half-hour, I must have found the missing wallet. So they paid me a visit, Bob waiting outside in case I'd seen him leaving the flat and might recognise him, Frank waving a gun at me on the stairs. When Frank didn't come out but I did, Bob trailed me to the Embankment, and it was then that he tried to run me down. After that he went back to Gresham Terrace to rescue his brother. And the rest you know."

"So it *was* the Webbs, and they *weren't* telling us the truth," said Olivia slowly. "And to think they had me prisoner," she shivered. "And yet – " she paused – "the statements they gave us tallied so exactly."

"Once they knew you were on their trail they guessed there might be trouble," said Rollison. "So they concocted their story. Half truth, half lies – it sounded more authentic that way. It all seems so obvious now – but if

Stride hadn't talked, and if the police hadn't found that wallet —"

"Oh well, you'd still have saved Madam Melinska," cried Olivia happily, "and after all, the rest doesn't really matter, does it? By the way, what made you think it might have been Mona who had the money?"

"A false clue, actually," admitted Rollison. "Or at least, a clue to the murder of Mrs. Abbott, and not to the missing money — only I didn't realise it."

"What was the clue?" demanded Olivia.

"Mona's diamond brooch and ear-rings. And bracelet. They cost a good three thousand between them, and I couldn't see Stride, or even Mike Fraser, giving them to her. In point of fact they were presents from her aunt, who had a great deal of jewellery. Had I known about this I'd have realised there was another motive for murder besides the dossier."

"Well, it's all sorted out now," said Olivia. "Has Mona gone back to Rhodesia with Madam Melinska?"

Rollison shook his head. "No, Madam Melinska went on her own. Mona's staying with Michael Fraser's secretary Jane — I told you that Mona and Michael used to be engaged, didn't I?"

Olivia nodded.

"They make a nice-looking couple," Rollison added genially. "I shouldn't be surprised —"

"What an old match-maker you are," laughed Olivia, interrupting him. "Just like a Virgoan. But it's no use trying to change you. Anyway —" she lifted her glass to him — "here's to you, the way you are."

JOHN CREASEY

One of the major factors in John Creasey's ever increasing popularity is undoubtedly his talent for viewing and so portraying his characters as living beings: each with his own special problem, each with his own hopes and dreams and fears. John Creasey has now written nearly 500 books, and in essence this extraordinary achievement is a testament to his penetrating observation and understanding of human behaviour. Criminals, their victims, the police – all he writes of are touched with this very real compassion.

He has long been noted for his use of sociological and industrial backgrounds (*A Gun For Inspector West* – 1953, and *Death In Cold Print* – 1961, are typical examples), portraying each with meticulous accuracy while demonstrating how the life of any man, in any walk of life, may be affected by the activities of criminals hitherto unknown to him. As his researches deepened his lifelong interest in social and political affairs, he soon turned part of his great energy to campaigning for National Savings, United Europe (1945–50), Road Safety, Oxfam and other national and local causes. Simultaneously, he took a close interest in politics, serving the Liberal Party with characteristic enthusiasm for over thirty years.

Despite all this, he has still found time to travel very widely and that innate power of observation — and a strong streak of idealism — quickened his interest in world poverty and world problems. The more he saw, the more he became aware of the interdependence of people everywhere — and the more convinced he became that failure to recognise this interdependence was the cause of most of the social, economic and political evils of the world.

(This theme — that it is Mankind's destiny to work together for the common good — has indeed been a feature of two of his finest series: the "police procedural" *Gideon*s and the later *West*s.)

It was a natural step for him to apply his beliefs to the British scene. And almost single-handed, he started a political movement — All Party Alliance — the purpose of which is to get the best men from all the parties working together in government. It is characteristic of Creasey that he spends a very large proportion of his income on this movement, besides publishing* a monthly journal — *A P A News* — in an effort to spread the ideas in which he believes and by which he works and lives.

*From 19 Coton Road, Nuneaton, Warwicks.